THE BEEKEEPER

A gripping crime mystery with a dark twist

STEWART GILES

JOFFE
BOOKS

Published 2017 by Joffe Books, London.

www.joffebooks.com

This book is a work of fiction. Names, characters, businesses, organizations, places and events are either the product of the author's imagination or are used fictitiously. Any resemblance to actual persons, living or dead, events or locales is entirely coincidental. The spelling is British English.

ISBN-13: 978-1-912106-51-6

For Ann & Keira.

'Remove the bee from the earth and at the same time you remove at least one hundred thousand plants that will not survive.' Attributed to Albert Einstein

CHAPTER ONE

"There's something wrong with the honey," Alice Green told her pet jackdaw.

The honey was sticky and golden brown as always. But after thirty years of beekeeping, Alice knew honey. She wasn't sure what had caused the change. The roses, peonies and hollyhocks had blossomed at the same time as last year and the bees had performed remarkably well. Yet this batch was off, somehow. She was sure of it.

Maybe I'm coming down with a cold or something, Alice thought. Her best friend Milly had just got over one. *Maybe I've caught something and it's affecting my taste buds.*

She looked at the jars on the huge oak table in the kitchen. Eighty-six jars of prized honey were ready to be taken to the Saturday market in Berryton. She wondered if anybody would be able to taste the difference.

Probably not. Cornwall was full of tourists at this time of year, and most of them probably never even opened the jars they bought. It was worth taking the risk. She wasn't going to throw away eighty-six jars at £7 each.

Alice jumped as the jackdaw let out a loud shriek. She had rescued the bird from the old railway line close to St Agnes a few years earlier. It would never fly again because its wings had been damaged beyond repair but it didn't seem to mind living in a cage. She fed it three times a day and its cage had a view over the back garden, with the Atlantic far in the distance. She liked the jackdaw's company. Her husband Stanley had left on one of his soul-searching adventures ten years ago and had never returned.

She opened the cage door and the jackdaw immediately hopped to the bottom.

"Clever boy." Alice scraped the remaining chunks from a tin of dog food onto the floor of the cage. The jackdaw eyed the food suspiciously, as it always did, and started to eat. "You don't trust anybody do you, boy?" Alice said. "Probably for the best." Funnily enough, she had never given him a name, she just thought of him as "the jackdaw," and that seemed fine.

The kitchen door opened and Milly Lancaster came in carrying a tray of eggs. Feathers were still stuck to the shells.

"Looks like I'm just in time." Milly eyed the jars of honey on the table.

"How's the cold?" Alice asked.

"Much better."

"Sit down and taste this." Alice spread some honey on a piece of bread. "Well?" she asked as Milly chewed.

"It's fine," Milly said eventually. "Really."

"No, there's something different. It's got an aftertaste I can't quite put my finger on."

"Have the bees strayed at all?"

"Not that I know of." Alice handed Milly a mug of tea. "My bees are Italian. They're lazy. They don't do anything unless they really have to."

"It's fine, honestly."

Alice was sure she was just being polite. "Maybe the next batch will be better. I'm taking it to Berryton tomorrow, all the same. The tourists won't know the difference. I doubt they even eat it anyway. It'll probably sit on the shelves in their fancy London kitchens, gathering dust."

"You're probably right," Milly agreed. She picked up one of the jars of honey and examined it. "It looks the same. And honestly, I can't taste any difference."

It took them an hour to pack up the honey in boxes of twelve, ready for the market the next day.

"D'you want these?" Alice asked, picking up the two leftover jars. "For your efforts, and for the eggs?"

"I still have some of the last batch left. Besides, you know I'm always happy to help."

She obviously didn't want it. Alice was sure Milly thought it was off.

"I suppose I can always use it in my baking," Milly conceded at last.

"I'm going to see to the bees," Alice said, changing the subject. "It's getting cooler outside, so they ought to be quite sluggish."

She was right. The bees were slowly getting ready to turn in for the night. Six boxes were stacked on top of each other under the shade of an old oak tree. Alice slid the lid off the top box and carefully removed one of the beeswax frames. She held it up to the sun to examine it more closely. The bees clung to the sheet, barely moving. Tiny dots of honey had appeared in the combs. The bees were already busy with their next batch.

"Everything seems fine." She put the frame back. "I still don't understand why the honey tastes different."

The garden certainly looked magnificent. The roses against the fence were in full bloom. Red, pink and white flowers hung from thick stems. Bumblebees clumsily bashed into the flowers. The rainwater from the previous evening's storm had settled on the inside of the petals.

"Your hollyhocks are doing beautifully." Milly came up and ran her fingers over the leaves.

"The bees love them. I think those and the roses give the honey its special flavour."

They were just about to go back in when Alice spotted something catching the sun beneath the clump of hollyhocks. It appeared to be metallic.

"What's that?" Milly had seen it too. She crouched down to take a closer look. "It looks like a ring. It's half-buried in the soil. I wonder how it got there."

Alice almost pushed her friend out the way in her haste to get to the ring. She tried to pick it up, but it wouldn't budge. She took a shovel and jabbed down on it. With one blow, the finger was severed from the hand.

Alice picked it up. There was a wedding ring on the finger. And though one gold band looks much like another, the finger it was still attached to was unmistakeable. Its tip was missing, just like her husband Stanley's.

Alice dropped the finger in disgust. Milly had fainted. She was lying on the grass, stone-cold unconscious.

CHAPTER TWO

Alice gazed at the stubby finger lying on the soil. Milly was starting to stir, so she had to think quickly. Alice picked up the grisly finger and tried to pull the gold band off. It wouldn't budge. Stanley's fingers had got thicker over the years.

"What on earth are you doing?" Milly was upright again, staring at Alice.

"Alice," Milly gasped, "What's going on?"

"I don't know." Alice put the severed digit in her pocket. "I really don't know what's going on. But I do know that nobody must find out about this."

"We need to phone the police, now!" Milly said, almost shrieking. "There's a dead . . . finger in your garden. The police need to know."

"Not yet. Not until I've had a chance to think things over. I'll phone them after the weekend."

"What's going on, Alice?" Milly eyed her friend. "Do you know whose finger that is? The ring looked vaguely familiar."

"I don't know. I don't know whose finger it is."

"We have to phone the police."

"Not yet," Alice said, much more loudly than she intended. Milly flinched. She tried to sound calmer. "Not yet. What harm can a few days do? I can't have every policeman in Cornwall digging up my garden the weekend of the market. I can't afford it. I've got eighty-four jars of honey to sell. I need the money."

Milly shook her head. "I don't like this, Alice. We need to phone the police."

"Please." Alice put her hand on her oldest friend's shoulder. "How long have we known each other?"

"Years." Milly was shaking.

"You were my maid of honour. You know me better than anybody else. Please just keep this between us until after the weekend. I'll phone the police first thing Monday morning. I promise."

Alice calmly filled the hole the finger had left. The last remaining bees were now leaving the flowers and were heading back to the safety of the hives.

"This will be our secret," Alice said. "Nobody can find out about this until I phone the police on Monday."

Milly nodded her head unhappily. "I have to get going," she said. "I still have some more baking to do before tomorrow."

"I'll see you at the market." Alice helped her up off the grass. "And remember what I said: not a word to anyone."

* * *

Alice stood by the sink and took the finger out of her pocket. It was dirty, rigid and had a blue tinge. Where it had been severed, it was treacle black. She took some butter and rubbed it around the ring. After a few twists, it came loose and dropped into the sink with a metallic ping. Alice ran some water into the sink, cleaned the soil off and examined it carefully. "S." and "A." and "14.6.75" were engraved on the inside of the ring. Stanley and Alice, 14

June 1975. Definitely that ring, then. She was wearing one just like it.

She thought back to her wedding day, that Saturday morning in the tiny registry office in Plymouth. It had been just the four of them: Alice, Stanley, Milly and Dennis Albarn, Stanley's good-for-nothing best man.

Best man? Alice shook her head. Dennis Albarn had been *the worst* thing that had ever happened to Stanley. Dennis had been Stanley's wingman during all the womanising. And she'd put up with it for thirty years. Thirty years of waiting at home, wondering if her husband would come back this time. And finally, ten years ago, Stanley had gone and not come back.

Until now.

She put the ring on the draining-board and threw the severed finger into the jackdaw's cage. The bird sniffed it suspiciously and then started to peck at it. Alice began writing the labels for the honey jars.

Seven pounds a jar. No, let's make it ten. Tourists would pay that for organic honey. That would make the total £840. Enough to see her through the rest of the month. She might even have enough left over to buy the huge television set she had her eye on. Her old television was tiny and her eyes weren't getting any younger. The one she wanted was in a second-hand shop in Trotterdown.

By the time she had finished writing and gluing on the labels, it was starting to get dark. The wind had picked up, and the feathers on the tray of eggs were moving in the breeze from the kitchen window. The jackdaw cawed. It was time for his supper. She opened a fresh tin of dog food and scraped a few chunks onto the bottom of the cage. The finger lay there, stripped to the bone. Alice picked up what was left of it and dropped it down the sink. She ran the garbage disposal system, which growled noisily, and it was gone.

She poured herself a glass of port and looked out the window at the back garden. A few drops of rain hit the roof and she shivered. She closed her eyes and offered a silent prayer to whoever was listening.

Please, please don't let it rain so much that it shifts the soil under the hollyhock bushes.

CHAPTER THREE

Market day dawned cloudless and still. Despite all that had happened the day before, Alice's mood was equally untroubled. It was a trick she had learned years before during one of Stanley's disappearances. Every night she closed her eyes, went through the preceding day step by step, faced down any demons she might have met along the way, and dropped off into a dreamless sleep from which she always awoke refreshed.

The jackdaw was making strange sneezing sounds in the kitchen as Alice went in. She smiled. Milly had come over a few days ago with her terrible cold, and the bird was now imitating her rather accurately. She fed him some more dog food and switched the kettle on. While the water was coming to the boil, she opened the back door and looked outside. Her cheerful mood chilled abruptly when she saw the rain gauge indicating that three inches of rain had fallen overnight.

She stepped outside onto the sodden grass and made her way past the beehives to the hollyhock bushes. She took a deep breath and looked directly at the soil by them. The rain had washed away a substantial amount of earth, and a bluish-black human hand was sticking out of the soil.

The ring finger, of course, was missing. Alice fought back the urge to vomit and tried to calm herself. She heard a disturbing sound from the kitchen and jumped. The jackdaw was sneezing again. She fancied she could hear her own heartbeat drumming too.

Alice scrabbled in the earth, scooping up piles of soil to cover the hand. She smoothed over the loose pile of dirt and stood on it. She felt something give as the hand was pushed deeper into the ground. She went back into the kitchen to wash her hands and finally drink her tea. The day had barely started but she already felt drained.

* * *

The drive to Berryton usually only took ten minutes, but in June the tourists jammed up the roads, and she had to leave more time. She got there for eight thirty and started to set up her stall. Usually Milly would have been there by now.

Milly's baking stall was one of the market's most popular attractions.

"Where's Milly?" Derek asked Alice. Derek had the stall next to hers. He sold Cornish pasties, which the tourist couldn't get enough of, even though Alice thought his pastry wasn't up to scratch.

"I haven't seen her. Maybe she's running late. The traffic was terrible this morning. She's going to lose her spot if she's not here soon."

* * *

That market day in Berryton turned out to be Alice's best yet. The green money tin was overflowing with notes and coins. That lot would easily see her through to the end of the month. She was still debating whether she would get that new television set. Everybody had seemed to enjoy the honey samples she had put out, whether or not they noticed the flavour had changed, and nobody had quibbled at the higher price. She threw the empty boxes into the back of the van and put the cash tin on the passenger seat in the front.

"See you next month, my love," Derek said.

I'm not your love and you're not even from Cornwall originally.

"See you next month, Derek. I'm going to see if Milly's all right."

"Maybe she just forgot. None of us are getting any younger."

"Perhaps." Alice got in the van and started the engine.

Milly Lancaster's house was two doors down from Alice's. It was a small cottage desperately in need of some work. The white paint had turned an off-yellow colour and was flaking off. Weeds had taken over the garden. Her husband Graham had maintained it when he was alive. After his death from a stroke a few years ago, the house and garden had gone to ruin.

Alice opened the rusty garden gate and pushed her way through the huge dock leaves that blocked the path. She rang the bell. There was no sound. It was obviously broken. She knocked harder and the door opened slightly. It was unlocked.

"Milly," she shouted, "Are you all right?"

There was no sound from inside. Alice pushed the door open and went in. The familiar smell of baking hung in the air. Milly's cakes, shortbreads and biscuits were famous for miles around. In the kitchen, rows of biscuits lay on cooling racks next to the open window. Three chocolate cakes stood on the table, ready to be sliced. Milly was nowhere to be seen.

"Milly," Alice shouted again.

There was only one bedroom in the small cottage. Alice went in. The bed was made and the window was open. *No Milly.* Alice checked the bathroom. Milly's toothbrush was in a glass next to the sink and nothing looked disturbed.

Milly Lancaster had got up and made her bed. Her baking was laid out ready to be packed for market. Alice felt queasy. She sat down at the table in the kitchen. For a moment she didn't know where she was. All she knew was that Milly was gone.

CHAPTER FOUR

Alice phoned the police, as she'd promised Milly. However, when she was finally put through to a rather grumpy-sounding constable in Trotterdown, she didn't mention Stanley's finger. She was more concerned about reporting Milly's disappearance, even though PC Wood tried his best to assure her that her friend would turn up soon enough. A few hours' absence didn't justify opening a missing person's case.

"But it's not like Milly," Alice argued. "She never misses the market. Her door was unlocked and her cakes were ready. Something's wrong."

"I'm sure it's nothing to worry about. Mrs Lancashire will turn up in the end."

"Lancaster."

"Excuse me?"

"Mrs Lancaster," Alice said. "Her name is Milly Lancaster. How are you going to find her when you can't even get her name right?"

She hung up.

"Idiot," the jackdaw screamed. "Idiot. Idiot."

"You're not wrong there, my boy," Alice told him. "This isn't like Milly. It isn't like her at all."

She needed something to take her mind off things. She opened up the green cash tin and took out £250. A new television set and a bottle of fine port would do the trick. She checked on the bees before setting off for Trotterdown. Normally, she wore protective gloves to open the hives when the sun was so high in the sky, but today she didn't even think about it. She lifted the lid off one of the hives and slid out one of the frames. There was much more honey on the frame than yesterday. The bees were performing magnificently.

A sharp pain on the back of her hand reminded her of the downside of beekeeping. She pulled the bee off, but its sting remained in her skin. "Why did you do that?" She dropped it on the ground and watched as it writhed on the floor, turning circles on its back. It was doomed. When she could take it no longer, she stepped on the poor creature.

The initial sharp pain on her hand had been replaced with a dull itch. She went back into her kitchen, and took a pair of tiny tweezers out of the drawer, along with a bottle of a baking soda solution she had made up for stings. She tweezed out the sting and applied a small amount of the baking soda. She tried to remember the last time she had been stung. It had been August last year, during a particularly nasty heatwave. As she'd told Milly, her bees were Italian, generally docile and not prone to sting on a whim.

* * *

Alice parked her van in the car park of the main shopping centre in Trotterdown. The itchiness from the sting had gone completely. She locked the van and patted her pocket. The money for a television set was safely there. The set she'd been eyeing in the second-hand shop for weeks was gone, but they had a perfectly good alternative for £20 less. By the time she drove back towards Polgarrow, she had almost forgotten about Milly. She was looking forward to watching her favourite quiz shows on the huge television. She wouldn't have to sit so close anymore to read the questions on the screen. And she was able to set it up. She'd learned to do all those things for herself over the past ten years on her own.

Alice was enjoying a rewarding glass of port and contemplating the evening's viewing when she heard a knock at the door. Only Milly would visit at this time of day and she never knocked. Alice sighed. She put the glass of port on the coffee table next to her armchair and got up to answer. *Maybe it was something to do with Milly?*

Eddie Sedgwick, the man who lived between Alice and Milly, was standing in the doorway wearing the most ridiculous sweater Alice had ever seen. It was bright green and it had a crudely embroidered white sheep in the centre.

"Eddie," Alice said. "What can I do for you?"

"Sorry to bother you, Alice, but the wife is moaning about the bees again. She reckons they're coming in our garden. Acting all aggressive, she says."

Alice couldn't help laughing at the idea of the bees "acting all aggressive." She pictured them buzzing around next door, getting up to no good and threatening the Sedgwicks with God knows what.

"Sorry, Eddie," she managed, composing herself at last. "I'll have a word with them. They're not normally aggressive. They're Italian bees."

"To be honest, they don't bother me in the slightest, but my Barbara reckons she's allergic."

"Tell Barbara not to worry. I'll sort them out." She closed the door in Eddie Sedgwick's face before he had a chance to say anything else.

"Idiot," the jackdaw screamed as Alice sat back down in the living room.

"All men are idiots," Alice said.

She leaned back in her chair to watch a new quiz show, glass of port back in her hand. Perhaps she ought to check to see if Milly was home — but maybe she'd leave it for now.

The quiz show was a huge disappointment. It was one of those contests where so-called celebrities tried their best to show off their wit. Alice had never even heard of any of the contestants. She changed the channel. The weather forecast had just started. A high-pressure front was arriving from the south. Warm temperatures were promised for the next few days.

"The bees are going to love that," Alice said to herself.

CHAPTER FIVE

The following morning, after checking on the bees, Alice went to Milly's cottage. The curtains were open, but then Alice knew Milly was an early riser. She always had been. She went in without knocking and realised straight away that her friend wasn't there.

Everything was exactly as it had been the day before, but flies were now buzzing around the biscuits and cakes in the kitchen. And again, Milly was nowhere to be seen.

Alice picked up Milly's telephone and called the police. *Surely they have to take things seriously now.* She was put through to a young-sounding woman with a peculiar accent. Definitely not Cornish.

"I wish to report a missing person," Alice said emphatically.

"Name?" the woman asked.

"Mine or hers?"

"Yours," the woman said. "Please could I have your name?"

"My name's Alice Green. My friend Milly Lancaster hasn't been seen since Friday evening. It's not like Milly. Something's happened to her. I reported it yesterday, but the man I spoke to didn't seem to give a damn."

"I'm sorry about that, Mrs Green," the woman said. She asked for the address and told Alice that someone would be along to see her "in the course of the morning."

Finally. Finally somebody is taking this seriously. People got away with murder these days. She went back to her own house. The bees were starting to surface as the temperature rose. Alice watched as they lazily left the hives, sunned their wings and flew off in search of nectar. None of them appeared to show any interest in the garden next door. Barbara Sedgwick and her allergies were safe for the time being. The bees were concentrating all their attention on the hollyhock bushes. More flowers had opened and the bees were enjoying them. It was all very peaceful.

Alice suddenly realised what was really happening. She had to think fast. The police were on their way to her house — and there was a body buried in her garden. Whether or not it was attracting the bees, she had to make sure they didn't check any further. She checked the soil round the hollyhocks. It was starting to harden in the sun and there was no sign of anything untoward.

"Mrs Green?" a man called out, making Alice jump. She turned to see a man and a woman standing a few metres from the hives. The man looked nervous.

"We did knock," the woman said. "The door was open so we came straight in. Are you Mrs Green?"

Alice recognised the woman's accent from the phone.

"Call me Alice."

"DS Duncan," the man said. "And this is my colleague, DC Taylor. Are those things dangerous?" He pointed to the beehives.

"Not at all," Alice said, "they're Italian. Have you ever known the Italians to be dangerous? Since the Romans, I mean."

The joke appeared lost on the middle-aged detective sergeant, but DC Taylor smiled. "What beautiful hollyhocks," she said, taking one of the flowers in her hand and smelling it. Alice could feel her heart starting to beat more quickly. The woman was standing just a few feet from her dead husband.

"The bees seem to like them," Alice said, moving towards the house. "Would you like some tea?" She went inside without waiting for an answer and they had no alternative but to follow her.

"When did you last see Mrs . . ." DS Duncan fumbled in his pocket for his notebook.

"Lancaster." Alice saved him the effort. "Milly Lancaster. I last saw her on Friday evening. She helped me pack the honey to take to the market."

"Market?" DS Duncan wrote it in his notebook.

"The market in Berryton. Milly and I have had stalls there for donkeys' years."

"I see." Duncan looked up. "What do you sell there?"

"I sell my honey and Milly takes her baking. Cakes, biscuits, that sort of thing. What's this got to do with it?"

"I'm just trying to get all the facts, Mrs Green." Duncan scribbled something in his notebook.

Alice heard the jackdaw's cage rattle and she flinched. She had a terrible feeling about what was coming next. She cast the bird a stern glance and he kept quiet.

"Right," Duncan read through his notes, "you say Mrs Lancaster helped you pack the honey on Friday evening? What time was this?"

"Around seven."

"And you haven't seen her since?"

"No." Alice was starting to get annoyed. "She didn't show up for the market and it doesn't look like she's been home. Something's happened to her."

"Let's not be premature here. I know it's worrying, but we know that most people who are reported missing turn up in the end. And there's often a perfectly reasonable explanation for their disappearance."

"What about the ones who don't?"

"Does Mrs Lancaster have any family?" Duncan ignored her question. "Friends she may have gone to visit without you knowing?"

"Her husband died a good few years ago. She has no children and, as far as I'm aware, I'm her only friend."

DC Taylor looked as if she was itching to say something. Alice nodded to her, pleading. She was getting a headache from DS Duncan's stupid questions.

"I think it might be an idea to check Mrs Lancaster's house, even so. This lady's clearly worried," Taylor suggested.

"All in good time," Duncan replied. Alice and DC Taylor both sighed at the same time.

* * *

After twenty minutes of irrelevant questioning DS Duncan stood up and told Alice — as if he'd thought of it for himself — that it would be a good idea to have a look inside Milly's house.

"Have you got a licence for that thing?" He pointed to the jackdaw.

"He can't fly anymore," Alice said. "He would've died if I hadn't taken him in."

"That's neither here nor there. If I'm not mistaken, you need a licence to keep wild birds. I'll be sure to check."

Alice, DS Duncan and DC Taylor had barely reached the front door when the jackdaw let rip.

"Idiot," the jackdaw squawked. "Idiot." Alice saw DC Taylor was trying hard not to laugh.

"He doesn't like men," she whispered to the detective constable. Taylor smiled and followed Alice outside to Milly's house.

DS Duncan insisted on taking the lead. Even more annoyingly, he spotted the biscuits on the tray in the kitchen and decided it was OK to try one. "Not bad," he said, spraying crumbs everywhere.

"I checked the house yesterday," Alice said. "And again this morning. Milly isn't here."

"Please just let us do our job." Duncan marched through the small cottage to the bathroom. "We've been specially trained in matters such as these."

I bet you have. When was the last time anyone went missing round here?

Duncan returned a few seconds later with a toothbrush and a triumphant look. "She's not here," he said. "I reckon if she was planning on going away for a few days she'd have taken her toothbrush with her. I think something is wrong."

Alice gritted her teeth.

"Let's start the ball rolling then, shall we?" Duncan put the toothbrush down on the table and picked up another biscuit. "Taylor, you stay here and get a statement from Mrs Green. Make sure you capture the whole chain of events. I'm going back to Trotterdown. I'll arrange for someone to check the local hospitals."

He looked at Alice and clearly felt he should try to sound sympathetic. "Just routine," he said, "like I said, she's almost certainly OK."

"Let's get started then, Sarge."

"If you need me," Duncan replied, "I'll be in the Unicorn in Trotterdown. I promised the wife a Sunday lunch out."

CHAPTER SIX

"Let's start from the very beginning, then," DC Harriet Taylor said.

"I don't mean to sound rude," Alice said, not particularly caring whether she did, "but that Duncan bloke isn't all there, is he?"

"DS Duncan is just very meticulous." Taylor took out a sheet of paper from a black file and started to write.

"Mrs Green," she said.

"Please call me Alice. Nobody calls me Mrs Green. Especially since my Stanley did a runner. If you don't mind me asking, dear, you're not from around here, are you? That accent. It's Scottish, isn't it?"

"Edinburgh. I transferred to Trotterdown six months ago. You last saw Milly Lancaster at around seven on Friday. Is that correct?"

"Round about then. What with the long days at this time of year, it's hard to say."

"And Mrs Lancaster seemed fine to you?"

"Yes. She always does."

"Do you know if anything was bothering her?"

"No," Alice said again. "She seemed fine to me."

"And she didn't mention anything about going away for a few days?"

"Nothing. And she'd have told me, I can promise you that. Like I said, we were planning on meeting up at the market the next day. Milly had her biscuits and cakes laid out ready to pack. You saw them yourself."

"Sorry, but I have to go through all these questions. We'd rather repeat ourselves than miss something. So — there was definitely nothing troubling her? Nothing's happened in the past few days that you can think of? Even something minor? "

Apart from seeing my dead husband's hand sticking up under my hollyhocks? "No," she repeated. "She seemed fine. How many times are you going to ask me the same question?"

"Sorry. I just need to make absolutely sure. You were right to let us know," Taylor said, "I don't normally like to sound alarmist, but it is a bit odd, particularly at her age. Could you read through this statement and sign it, please?"

Taylor had been very thorough and she'd got everything in order, but there wasn't anything irrelevant either. "Everything seems fine." She signed her name at the bottom of the page. "What happens next?"

"We follow the usual procedures." Taylor put the statement back in the file. "We see what we find from the hospitals, speak with the neighbours, all that. We'll look for anything out of the ordinary that might explain Mrs Lancaster's sudden disappearance."

"Such as?"

"You'd be surprised. In Edinburgh last year a seventy-two-year-old man went missing. Disappeared into thin air. When we dug further, we found out from his bank accounts that he'd won the lottery. He didn't want his wife finding out. We tracked him down to the south of Spain. He's back home with his wife now, funnily enough — he couldn't cope on his own."

"Men," Alice said. "They're all the same."

"We'll be in touch, Mrs Green." Taylor held out a slender hand. Alice grasped it tightly.

"And please," Taylor added, "please let us know if your friend does show up."

After DC Taylor had left, Alice sat in the kitchen and looked out onto the back garden. The bees were at their busiest now, buzzing back and forth between the flowers and the hives.

Milly hasn't won the lottery. She isn't sitting on a beach in Spain right now, wondering how to spend her money.

She couldn't remember if Milly even played the lottery. She remembered the first time they'd met though. It was a summer dance in Plymouth. They were both eighteen years old but Alice seemed years ahead in confidence and experience. Milly had always been the shy, nervous one. While Alice flirted, Milly would always be in the background waiting for something to happen. Alice always thought it was a miracle Milly ever got married.

She'd met Stanley at another Plymouth dance too. Handsome, charming Stanley Green. She ought to have known from the start how it would all turn out. She should have known those blue eyes and crooked smile were trouble.

Alice poured herself a glass of port. It was a bit early but she needed something to calm her nerves. It had been a trying few days. First the finger, and now her best friend had disappeared. The jackdaw started to make a droning sound which was distinctly like the dull detective sergeant.

"Don't be cheeky." Alice opened the cage and scraped some dog food onto the tray on the bottom. "You jackdaws will eat anything, but you do love your dog food. But this 'idiot' business has got to stop. Do you hear me?" The phone rang as she closed the cage door.

"Mrs Green," said DC Taylor, "sorry to bother you."

"Have you found something?"

"I'm sorry, but not at the moment. I just wanted to ask you something. You said you and Mrs Lancaster have been going to the market in Berryton for years."

"That's right."

"But you go there in different vehicles, even though you live just two doors away from each other? You told me you first became suspicious when she didn't turn up."

"We used to both go in my van. It's got more space in the back than Milly's car. But then Milly started to complain about my driving. She said it scared the life out of her and she reckoned I ruined most of her baking on the way. The van's old and it gives quite a bumpy ride."

"So Mrs Lancaster has her own car?"

"She's got a small Ford. One of those Fiestas, I think."

"I didn't see a car there earlier. Where does she keep it?"

"She parks it on the road by the pub. It's just down the road. The Old Boar. There's no place to park outside Milly's cottage." Parking in Polgarrow had always been a problem.

"Could you do me a favour? I'm stuck in Trotterdown for the next few hours. Could you check to see if Mrs Lancaster's car is still there?"

"Of course." Alice wrote down the police woman's mobile phone number on the pad by the phone and hung up.

Alice locked her front door and walked down the road to the pub. She passed the Old Boar and carried on towards the village store. She crossed the road and returned in the direction of her house. Milly's blue Ford Fiesta was nowhere to be seen.

CHAPTER SEVEN

DC Taylor and DS Duncan arrived at Alice's house just over an hour later. Duncan seemed unimpressed. He had changed his clothes, and was now wearing a golf shirt and a pair of black jeans. The smell of stale beer hit her in the face as he came in.

"This is a new development, of course," he told her. "Mrs Lancaster is missing and now so is her car. I'd say this puts an entirely new perspective on things."

"What do you mean by that?" Alice asked.

"Mrs Green," DC Taylor said, "DS Duncan seems to think this is a good sign."

"And what do you think, dear?" Alice said.

"She's taken her car and she's gone off somewhere," Duncan said before Taylor had a chance to answer. "We're checking for any reports of cars with that registration, but we know that nobody fitting Mrs Lancaster's description has turned up in any of the local hospitals. And from what you've said, there's nothing to suggest any funny business. Your friend will turn up when she's good and ready, Mrs Green. You mark my words." The alcohol on his breath was starting to make Alice feel ill.

"What do you think?" she asked Taylor again.

"DS Duncan is probably right," Taylor told her. "There's no evidence of foul play." She sounded carefully non-committal.

"We'll see ourselves out," Duncan said.

"Idiot." The jackdaw said.

"That reminds me," Duncan added. "I must remember to check on that wild bird licence business. First thing in the morning. Now I have to get back to my wife."

Alice watched as they drove away. Taylor's words hadn't exactly filled her with confidence. Something in her tone suggested she thought something had happened to Milly Lancaster.

Milly wouldn't just drive off into the sunset, she thought.

She poured herself a large glass of port and went into the back garden. The bees were ready to call it a day. Alice checked the hives one by one. They were doing well. If they continued like this, she would have double the normal amount to sell at the Berryton market next month.

She took a long sip of port and wandered over to the hollyhock bushes. She shivered when she thought about how close DC Taylor had been to the disturbed soil. She wondered how and why Stanley's hand had surfaced.

"Hello there." Eddie Sedgwick had been watching her from his garden.

Alice jumped. She wondered how long he had been standing there.

"Lovely day," Eddie said.

Alice glared at him. He was wearing a pair of denim shorts and a pink T-shirt with the words "I love Florida" on it. His legs were pale and hairless.

"Is everything all right?" he asked her. "I couldn't help but notice that the police have been round twice today. I recognised Sergeant Duncan. I know him from poker nights in Trotterdown."

"Everything's fine," Alice snapped. She stepped away from the hollyhock bushes.

"How do you get yours to bloom so nicely?" Eddie pointed to the hollyhocks. "Barbara's always moaning at me about ours. I only seem to get a few flowers each year. Are you using some kind of special fertiliser?"

"It's the bees. They help with the pollination."

"Well, tell your bees," Eddie looked around to make sure nobody was listening, "they're welcome in my garden any time." The pathetic grin on his face irritated her. Perhaps he thought he was being witty. "Bugger what my Barbara says," he added.

Eddie stood there for a few moments without saying anything. Alice tried to ignore the inane grin on his face.

"Must dash, then," he said eventually. "My Barbara will be sending out a search party."

Alice watched as he turned and walked up the path to his house. The Sedgwicks had lived next door to her for almost thirty years and Alice could count on the fingers of one hand how many times she had set foot in their house. The only neighbour she liked was Milly, and she'd disappeared. Something was definitely wrong. Milly was not the type to set off on a road trip without telling her best friend.

Alice went back in. The doorbell rang as she switched on her new TV. A sombre-looking DC Taylor stood there. It was pretty clear from her expression that she did not have good news.

"Sorry to bother you so soon," Taylor said. "Can I come in?"

"Have you found Milly?"

"Please," Taylor said, "can I come inside?"

Alice stepped aside.

"We've found Milly Lancaster's car." Taylor came straight to the point.

"What about Milly? Have you found Milly?"

"No. That's the thing. Mrs Lancaster wasn't in her car."

"That's good news then, isn't it? Where was the car?"

"That's what worrying us," Taylor said. "A hiker found the car. He was walking along the top of Merryhead when he spotted something."

"What on earth was Milly doing up on Merryhead?" Alice asked. It was a popular spot for young couples, but not for older local people. The view across the sea was spectacular but the cliffs were sheer. It was unwise to venture too close to the edge.

"The car wasn't up on the cliffs. It was smashed to pieces on the rocks below."

"Oh my God." Alice sat down. "Are you sure it was Milly's car?"

"Positive. The hiker had a pair of binoculars. Even though the car was pretty badly smashed up he managed to get a look at the registration number."

"And you're sure Milly's not inside?"

"We've got a team down there right now. They had their work cut out for them with the tide coming in, but they managed to get the car onto a trailer. There was no sign of her."

"But that's good news, surely?" Alice insisted.

"I'm not sure." Taylor refused to reassure her. "The way I see it, it can only mean one of two things."

"Two things?"

"Either Milly wasn't in the car when it went over the cliff or she was thrown out at the bottom and her body was washed out to sea. I don't mean to alarm you, Mrs Green, but I'm afraid you need to prepare yourself for the worst."

* * *

Alice stared at a spot of dirt on the wall above the fireplace. DC Taylor had promised to let Alice know if anything new came up. Milly's car was now in the hands of the forensics technicians and Taylor had assured Alice that they would go over the vehicle with a fine-toothed comb.

If Milly had been in the car when it plummeted onto the rocks, they would know soon enough.

Alice felt numb. They'd been best friends for so long. A flood of thoughts filled her head. She fought them off by thinking about the past.

She had been with Milly when her husband had died. At the time, Alice had been surprised at how strong Milly had been through it all and how soon she'd adapted to her new life. It was as if her husband had never been around at all. It was only when Stanley had left for the last time that Alice had finally understood how Milly felt. Life was so much easier without a husband to fret about.

She poured a glass of port, sat back in the chair and took a large gulp. It made her feel light-headed. She closed her eyes . . . and quickly opened them again when an image of her husband filled her head. He was smiling his boyish smile, with the chipped tooth gleaming white in the corner of his mouth.

My husband lies buried in my garden, and now my best friend's broken body is lying cold at the bottom of the sea. What a horrible turn of events.

She finished her glass of port and poured herself another one. The bottle was nearly empty.

"What now, Alice Green?" she said out loud.

She raised the glass in the air. She was feeling very tipsy now.

"To absent friends," she said, "Milly Lancaster and you, Stanley Green, you bastard."

She drained the glass and placed it carefully on the coffee table. She closed her eyes and drifted off to sleep.

CHAPTER EIGHT

DC Harriet Taylor parked outside her house. There was nothing more they could do until the forensic investigators had finished going over Milly Lancaster's car.

She found some ginger beer lurking in the back of her fridge and took a glass outside to the back garden. The wind was blowing in from the west which meant a new weather front was on the way. The house was still new to her — she'd bought it without even viewing it in person. The photographs on the estate agent's website had sold it to her immediately. It was a three-bedroom detached house with different views of the Atlantic depending on which room you were in. Her neighbours were mostly middle class — and the peace and quiet suited Taylor just fine. She'd been lucky. When she had made the offer on the house, her head had not been quite right. It was three weeks after the accident which had turned her world upside down.

Taylor sat down on the garden bench and breathed in the crisp sea air. She thought about the day of the accident. She remembered it as clearly as if it had been yesterday. Probably she always would. It had been the fifth of November, Guy Fawkes Night. It had been cold and damp, as it always was in Edinburgh in November, and Taylor had been called out to investigate a burglary. Fireworks were going off all around the city and the air was thick with smoke and the stench of sulphur. Other than that, it had a been a pretty ordinary evening.

When she got back to the station, nobody would look her in the eye. Had she done something wrong? If so, she had no idea what. Eventually, Inspector Morag Childes, a hulking mass of a woman, appeared and asked Taylor into her office.

The look in Childes' eyes was something Taylor would never forget. She remembered the conversation in that office word for word.

"Take a seat," Childes had said.

"What's going on?" Taylor sat down. "Everybody around here is treating me like I have the plague."

Childes looked out of the window. A huge bang went off and the sky lit up with red, blue and green light.

"There's been an accident down on the Lothian Road," Childes said to the window.

"An accident?"

"A lorry hit a car head on. The people in the car didn't stand a chance."

"That's terrible. But what's it got to do with me?"

"I'm afraid Daniel was driving the car."

She went numb at the sound of her husband's name. Daniel 'Danny' Taylor was a property developer in the city. They had been married for two years.

"Daniel was killed instantly," Childes continued. "The woman in the passenger seat died on the way to hospital."

It didn't take Taylor long to realise what had been going on. The woman in the car with Danny was a client — and she was not the first woman to go for a late-night drive in Danny's car. As Taylor dug a bit further and discovered the sordid details of Danny's cheating, the initial grief turned to anger and then pure hatred. Her husband had been playing around from before the time they were married. Everything suddenly fell into place — the late-night property viewings, all the evenings supposedly spent working. Danny had been making a fool out of her since the day they met.

When Taylor had finally returned to work after the funeral, things started to get worse. Underneath the sympathetic faces and hidden in the undertones of the kind words, something else was happening. Her colleagues were laughing at her. People she had risked her life with were now mocking her. Harriet Taylor, the policewoman who hadn't even realised her husband was having an affair.

In the end she had woken up one morning and decided enough was enough. She needed to get as far away from Edinburgh as possible. She started frantically searching through the jobs on the internal website and the DC post in Trotterdown was perfect. It was far enough away from the ghosts in Edinburgh, and a promotion to boot. Taylor begged Inspector Childes to recommend her for the post and Childes agreed. The insurance money from the accident more than covered the cost of the expensive house and Taylor had started her new life in Trotterdown in January that year.

And still, after six months, it still did not seem real. Growing up on one of the less desirable estates in Edinburgh, she would never have dreamed she would one day own a house like this. But then she wouldn't have expected quite a lot of the other things that had happened either.

This is all that's left of Danny Taylor, she thought, a house with a sea view and a heart full of hatred.

Her mobile phone rang, with a number on the screen she did not recognise. "We've got word from forensics," said her colleague DI Jack Killian. "I tried to get hold of Duncan but he's not answering his phone."

"He's at the Unicorn with his wife. What did they find?"

"They've gone over the whole car," Killian told her. "They've got some new diagnostic equipment they use these days and they found something interesting."

"Sir?"

"The handbrake was off when the car went over the edge and they reckon the engine was off too."

"What does that mean?"

"I'm not finished. All four doors were locked. Not just locked but jammed closed. Forensics could tell. They're not a hundred percent sure but the head technician reckons the woman was locked inside the car and then it was pushed over the cliff."

"Murdered?"

"Alan Littlemore doesn't usually make mistakes."

"What about the body?"

"There was definitely somebody in the car when it went over the edge. Littlemore reckons it went over nose first and hit the rocks at the bottom, and the woman was thrown out the windscreen on impact. They found traces of blood and hair on the broken glass. I've checked the tide tables — the car was jammed in the rocks but the tide could easily have washed the body of a woman out to sea. Milly Lancaster was not a large woman, by all accounts."

"So it was definitely Milly Lancaster?"

"We're not one-hundred-per-cent sure yet. We'll need a sample of her DNA to compare with what we got from the car."

"I can drive over to her house and bring in a hairbrush or toothbrush."

"It can wait until tomorrow. The tech guys haven't quite finished yet. I just wanted to fill you in on what we have so far."

"Thanks," Taylor said. "Murder. Are we any closer to any motive?"

"We've got nothing. Nasty, though, whatever it was."

She rang off and looked at the ominous bank of clouds forming in the west. Time for bed. She took out the pink pillbox she usually carried in her bag, shook two blue capsules into her hand and swallowed them with the last of the ginger beer. She had started taking the sleeping pills shortly after the accident and now she found she couldn't cope without the dreamless sleep they gave her. She knew that in half an hour or so, her eyes would start to feel heavy and her mind would slowly fill with dark mist. She put the pillbox back in her pocket and went upstairs to bed.

CHAPTER NINE

Taylor woke to the sound of her phone ringing beside her.

"There are two police cars outside Milly's house," Alice Green said without any preamble. "They've been there since early this morning."

"They're probably just having another look around."

"Have you found something?"

"We're not sure yet."

"Milly's dead, isn't she?"

"Like I said, we're not sure yet. We'll know more during the course of the day." She tried to sound as steady and reassuring as possible.

"I'm going to go over and ask them what they're doing."

"Please, Mrs Green, please just let them do their jobs. If anything turns up, I promise I'll let you know."

"Will you be popping round this morning? I'll make us some tea and we can have some honey and bread. The honey's a bit odd, but it's still good, you know."

"I have to go to work." Taylor looked at the clock on the microwave. She was going to be late already.

"Milly was my friend."

"I'll see if I have time to come by later." She felt obliged to — after all this was an old lady who'd lost one of the few people she was close to. "I have to go to work now, though."

The police station in Trotterdown was a far cry from the hovel Taylor had worked at in Edinburgh. The outside of the station was clean and fresh. Flower-boxes had been placed on each side of the entrance. The car park was almost full, for once, with unfamiliar cars. She realised why when she went inside the station.

Unsurprisingly, the story of a car going over the cliff at Merryhead had attracted reporters, who were now pestering PC Hargreaves at reception. "I don't have anything to tell you," Hargreaves insisted. "I'm just manning the front desk. I'm sure you'll all be informed in due time."

Taylor hated journalists. After Danny's accident in Edinburgh, they had hounded her day and night. One had even shown up at the funeral, complete with photographer. She despised the lot of them.

"Morning," Hargreaves said. He looked harassed. "The DI wants everybody in for a meeting at nine thirty."

"Is this about the car that went over the cliff?" asked a woman with a microphone. "Do we know if there was anybody in the car when it went over the edge?"

"Yes," Taylor said without thinking, "we do happen to know whether or not there was someone in the car at the time." She walked past them down the corridor. Hargreaves sniggered.

DI Killian was poring over some notes in the small meeting room. "There's a pack of wolves at the front desk," Taylor told him. "It doesn't take that lot long to sniff out a story."

"I'm afraid this is just the beginning. What happened up on Merryhead is going to be big news. You should know by now that nothing much usually happens around here."

"Can't we just kick them out?"

"I'm afraid not. In this day and age it's a case of quid pro quo. They can actually prove to be very useful."

"You can't be serious?"

"Press coverage helps us reach people we couldn't otherwise. Have you seen Duncan?"

"His car wasn't in the car park."

"He's probably hungover. You're not a drinker, are you?"

"Not much. I'm usually on the tonic water or ginger beer."

The door opened and PC Eric White and PC Thomas White walked in. They looked alike and shared the same surname, so everybody assumed incorrectly that they were related. "We can't wait all day for Duncan," Killian said. "We've got a lot to go through today. Taylor, you can start at the beginning for the benefit of the Whites."

"Milly Lancaster was reported missing on Saturday," Taylor started. "The PC who took the call didn't feel there was anything to be concerned about. Milly's friend Alice Green phoned in again yesterday. I took the call myself. DS Duncan and I went to take a statement and have a look around Milly's house. There was no sign of a disturbance and the only thing missing was Milly's car. As we all know, the car was found yesterday at the bottom of Merryhead,"

"Right." Killian glanced at his notes. "I have the initial forensics report right here. The brakes were off and the locks on the doors had been tampered with. They were jammed shut. The engine wasn't on when the car went over the edge."

"So someone pushed the car over the edge with Mrs Lancaster inside?" Thomas White said.

"It appears so, yes. There was blood on the shattered windscreen as well as strands of hair. We now have some hair samples from Mrs Lancaster's house and they're being analysed as we speak."

"If she was inside the car, what happened to her body?" Eric White asked.

"She was probably washed out to sea," Taylor suggested.

"Which may mean we'll never find her body," Killian pointed out. "The tide would have taken her right out." His phone started to ring in his pocket.

"Killian," he answered it. "Thank you." He put it back and frowned. "That settles it, then. The blood found on the windscreen belongs to Milly Lancaster. She was definitely in the car when it went over the edge of the cliff." He scratched at a scab on his nose.

"The missing person case is now a murder investigation," he added. "White and White, I want you to start gathering information about Milly Lancaster. We need to speak to everybody who might have spoken to her before she ended up on the rocks. We have to piece together her movements before the car was pushed over the cliff."

"Alice Green last saw her on Friday evening at around seven," Taylor said.

"Then we'll start there. You can speak to Mrs Green yourself. I'm going to liaise with our friends from the press. I want Milly Lancaster's photograph out on all media by tomorrow morning. Somebody must have seen something. An old lady doesn't just end up at the bottom of a cliff without somebody knowing something about it."

CHAPTER TEN

DC Taylor's heart was beating faster than normal as she drove to Polgarrow. *Murder,* she thought. *Finally, something to sink my teeth into.* Dreadful, of course, but also something she could get really involved in. Since she had transferred to Trotterdown, nothing she had worked on had sparked much interest. The odd housebreaking and a less than suspicious death of a ninety-year-old man had been the highlight of her time in the south-west so far. But now she had a murder to investigate.

Taylor parked outside Alice Green's house and stopped the engine. Alice opened the door before Taylor had even reached the path leading up to the house. "I knew you'd come," she said, smiling. "I'll put the kettle on. The bees have been busy too, so we can have fresh honey. I hope it's all right this time."

She seemed quite cheerful. Taylor felt slightly sick: how was she going to tell this nice old lady that her best friend had been pushed over a cliff in her car? She followed Alice through to the kitchen, where the jackdaw was preening the feathers of its broken wing in the cage by the window.

"I'm afraid I have some bad news." Taylor came straight to the point.

"Milly's dead, isn't she?" Alice put two tea cups on a tray along with some slices of bread and honey.

"I'm afraid so. It's been confirmed. She was inside the car when it went over the cliff. It looks like her body was washed out to sea."

"Oh my." Alice's face went pale. Taylor was afraid she was going to faint.

"I'm all right." Alice poured some hot water into a teapot, but her hands were shaking.

"Let me help you with that." Taylor took the tray from her. "I know this is hard, but I have to ask you a few more questions."

"Of course."

"You said you last saw Milly on Friday evening?"

"That's right. Milly helped me to pack the honey and she left around seven. She had to finish off some baking."

"And she seemed fine to you? There wasn't anything bothering her?"

"She was getting over a cold. That's all I can think of."

"And she didn't mention that something was troubling her?"

"No, and she would have. Milly tells me everything." Alice poured two cups of tea. Her hands had stopped shaking.

"Why are you asking me all this again?" she said. "You're not thinking she did herself in, are you?"

"No, there's no doubt about that. The car was helped over the edge."

"Somebody pushed her over a cliff?" Alice seemed shocked. "Who on earth would do such a terrible thing?"

"We don't know yet." Taylor took a sip of tea. "But we'll get to the bottom of all this, I promise."

They sat in silence for a while. The only sound in the kitchen came from the jackdaw's cage. It was frantically pecking one of its feet.

"Forty-two years," Alice said, "forty-two years I've known Milly Lancaster. She was at my wedding. Me and Stanley. A match made in heaven." She stared out of the window. "My arse," she added, "if you'll pardon my French."

"Where's your husband now?" Taylor asked.

"Stanley?" Alice looked slightly flustered. "Your guess is as good as mine. He walked out ten years ago. I haven't seen him since."

"I'm sorry."

"I'm not," Alice said. She sounded calmer again. "What about you? A pretty young girl like you must have somebody in your life."

"No, there's nobody."

"There will be, you mark my words, but watch out — all men are liars. They promise the world and they always let you down. Give me the bees any day. Did you know that a bee will die for his queen if he has to? Without even thinking twice about it. That's loyalty. No, men are worse than rats. Do you think the honey is all right? I still think it's tasting a little odd."

"Really, it seems fine to me. When Mrs Lancaster left your house on Friday, do you know if she went anywhere?"

"She headed straight home, I think. She needed to get ready for the market."

"And you didn't notice if she got in her car? You didn't see her drive off?"

"No, Milly always parks by the pub. If she was going up to Merryhead, she wouldn't have passed by my house anyway. Merryhead's in the opposite direction."

A knock on the door made the jackdaw rattle its cage.

"Who can that be now?" Alice stood up and went to the door. She returned a moment later with the two PC Whites in tow.

"We saw your car parked outside," Eric said to Taylor.

"We haven't found anything," Thomas White added. "It seems that Milly Lancaster kept herself to herself. She very rarely went out. She even had her groceries delivered."

"I could've told you all that," Alice said. "I'm Milly's best, and only, friend."

"Sorry," Taylor said, "these are two colleagues of mine. PCs Eric and Thomas White."

"White and White?" Alice stared at the two constables. "I can see the resemblance."

"What now?" Eric White asked Taylor, ignoring the observation he'd heard many times before.

"We leave Mrs Green in peace."

"My dad used to keep bees," said Thomas.

"Good for him," said Alice, showing them to the door.

* * *

Taylor stopped her car on the grass at the top of Merryhead and made sure the handbrake was on. Even though she had parked a good distance away from the edge of the cliff, the ground sloped down and the edge felt very near. She got out and gazed at the Atlantic. She could see a line of cargo vessels in the distance and the small silhouette of a sailing boat closer to land. The wind had torn down the police tape, and it now flapped loosely from metal poles. The forensic technicians had gone over every inch of where Milly Lancaster's car had been parked before it had gone over the cliff.

She wondered what had gone through Milly's mind as the car had started to roll towards the edge of the cliff. *What was it like to realise you have only a few seconds left to live?*

Inevitably, her thoughts drifted off to the day of her husband's accident. Her legs started to tremble and she had to sit down on the grass.

She stared out to sea and tried to regulate her breathing. She watched as a lone gull folded its wings and plummeted into the water. It surfaced a few seconds later empty-handed. She went on staring at the sea for quite some time. Eventually, she plucked up the courage to risk standing up again. *Concentrate*, she told herself, as she got to her feet slowly.

Her vision went blurry for a few seconds but soon steadied. She took a last look over the cliff and got back in her car.

CHAPTER ELEVEN

Alice Green finished reading the article about *Nosema Apis* in the *Beekeepers Quarterly*. It hadn't done anything to lift her spirits — whole colonies of bees were being wiped out by the disease and the author of the article believed the future of beekeeping looked bleak. She fed the jackdaw and went outside to the back garden.

Her heart almost stopped as she saw what had happened underneath the hollyhock bushes. It looked as if a wild animal, probably a fox, had dug up a large amount of the soil and now a dirty arm was clearly visible. Alice recognised the shirt the arm was wrapped in. It had been Stanley's favourite black-and-white checked shirt. He'd worn it for years.

This can't go on.

She wondered if it was time to tell the police — she had made a promise to Milly, after all — but then again it would only spell trouble. The police would start asking all kinds of questions, especially after what had happened to Milly.

No, Alice thought, *there's only one thing to do. Stanley's body must remain hidden, one way or another.*

She fetched the spade and started to dig next to the body. The bees buzzed around her head as she worked. When she had enough to cover the mess the fox had made, she shovelled the soil onto the exposed arm. It was only a temporary measure, of course. The fox was bound to come back. She would have to find some way to dig up her husband and dispose of his body for good, somewhere far away, but that would take a bit of careful planning, and she had neither the time nor the energy for that at the moment.

Satisfied that the corpse was suitably hidden, Alice set down the spade and wiped the sweat from her brow. She was exhausted.

"Beautiful day for it." Eddie Sedgwick appeared in the doorway. "I did knock but you obviously didn't hear. I've been meaning to get down to a bit of gardening myself." He looked at the freshly-dug earth underneath the hollyhock bushes.

"The bees are getting busier by the day." She had to think quickly. "I decided to plant some more hollyhocks."

"I wish ours grew like yours."

"Can I help you with something?" Alice could not face making small talk. She wondered how long Eddie had been standing there.

"We'd like to invite you over for supper." Eddie smiled. "It was actually my Barbara's idea. I couldn't believe it when she suggested it."

"When?" Alice was shocked.

"This evening. If it's convenient with you, that is."

It was the last thing Alice felt like but she agreed all the same.

"Come by around six," Eddie said, obviously very pleased with himself.

She had two hours before the supper ordeal. She hadn't mentioned Milly's death to Eddie, and she didn't intend to. It was none of his damn business. She was not looking forward to the dinner, but it might take her mind off everything that had happened in the past few days. She sat in her kitchen slumped over a cup of tea, looking at the door, half-expecting Milly to come shuffling in carrying a freshly-baked chocolate cake or a new batch of biscuits. It still did not seem real. Her oldest friend was now lying at the bottom of the sea.

"Stanley," the jackdaw shrieked. "Stanley Green."

Alice was shocked. She had taught the bird to say a lot of things, but her husband's name wasn't one of them.

"Now, where did you hear that?" She stared at the jackdaw. "You mustn't say that again. Do you hear me?" The bird pecked at the side of the cage in response.

At six, Alice made her way next door, armed with half a bottle of port. She had decided that if she was going to have to endure an evening with the Sedgwicks, she would need a bit of help. Eddie Sedgwick answered the door with his usual inane grin, which widened when he saw the bottle. "We'll definitely have a drop of that later."

He led her into the meticulously neat cottage. Alice could not remember the last time she had been inside but she remembered that Barbara Sedgwick had always been extremely house-proud.

"Take a seat," Eddie told her. "Barbara's just finishing off in the kitchen. What'll it be? Red or white?"

It could be green or pink for all I care. Just give me something to drink so I can make it through this. "You choose."

Eddie waltzed off and returned with a bottle of Riesling and two wine glasses.

"This ought to go nicely with the haddock." He poured Alice a glass. "My Barbara doesn't drink much since her operation, but that doesn't stop us, does it?" He poured himself a glass and sat down. "Cheers." He took a small sip and added, in a voice little more than a whisper. "Can you do me a favour? Don't talk about your bees. It's a bit of a sore topic at the moment, if you know what I mean."

"No bees," Alice agreed.

* * *

After producing the driest piece of haddock Alice had ever tried to swallow, Barbara returned to the kitchen to do the dishes. Alice and Eddie were left alone with the port.

"That was very nice," Alice lied. "Barbara's a very good cook."

"She used to be," Eddie poured them both a generous glass, "before the operation, I mean. I don't know what happened, but she hasn't been herself since then. She seems to have forgotten how to cook."

He looked around the room as if to make sure there were no hidden eavesdroppers.

"Between you and me," he whispered, "I couldn't take it any longer. After one piece of rubbery steak too many, I had to get my false teeth reinforced."

Alice started to laugh. She was beginning to see another side to her doddery next-door neighbour.

By the time the bottle of port was finished, the sun was starting to set. It was Alice's cue to make her excuses and leave.

"Thank you, Eddie." She stood up. "It was a lovely evening."

"We must do it again sometime," Eddie said. "I promise I'll cook next time."

Alice was about to go through to the kitchen to say her goodbyes to Barbara when there was an almighty scream. Eddie and Alice rushed through to the kitchen. Barbara Sedgwick was sitting at the table staring at the small television screen on the wall. She was very pale and her mouth was wide open. On the screen was a blown-up photograph of Milly Lancaster.

CHAPTER TWELVE

DC Taylor woke to the sound of the newspaper landing on the doormat downstairs. The letterbox was still rattling as she sat up in bed and rubbed her eyes. She had barely slept. After the episode up on Merryhead she had decided to see if one sleeping pill would be enough. It had been a bad idea. She had spent the night drifting between periods of semi-slumber and consciousness. After a while, she wasn't sure whether she was asleep or not.

The only sleep she'd had, included a vivid nightmare. She was in the car with her husband Danny. A truck came towards them in slow motion and she heard Danny scream. Just before impact, the face of the woman who Taylor had only seen in the mortuary filled her vision. Danny's bit on the side was smiling as she said, "You've been such a fool, Harriet Taylor."

Taylor went downstairs and picked up the newspaper. There was a photograph of Milly Lancaster on the front page. The details were rather vague — just that a car had gone over the cliff at Merryhead and an elderly woman was missing — but at the end there was the part she'd been dreading. The police were asking for "anybody who may have been in contact with Mrs Lancaster between Friday evening and Saturday night to come forward with any information they might have." The phone number underneath was the number for the switchboard at Trotterdown police station.

It was going to be a long day.

* * *

Half an hour later, when Taylor arrived at the station, a crowd of journalists was already gathered outside. She pushed through them, ignoring the shouting, and slammed the door with some difficulty. She made her way to her tiny office at the end of the corridor and sat down at her desk.

"It's going to be chaos for the next few days." DI Killian stood in the doorway. "The phones are already going crazy."

He came inside and walked up to the window.

"Look at them," he said, "even the nationals have got someone out there. We're going to have to be very careful with this one. Every move we make will be under the microscope."

"Has anybody reported anything useful?" Taylor asked.

"Mostly time-wasters, but that's to be expected, I'm afraid. Eric White thought he was onto something, but that one fizzled out. You look tired."

"I didn't sleep much last night. Too much on my mind. What's the plan for today?"

"We wait, we wait some more, and we see what comes in. Someone must have seen something. A car doesn't go over a cliff without someone noticing."

Killian was about to say something else when a very red-faced PC Thomas White barged in.

"Sorry to interrupt," he said, "but a man's just phoned in. A Peter Sugden. He reckons he spoke to Milly Lancaster on Friday night around eight."

"Where is he now?" Killian asked.

"At home. I got his address and contact number. I told him to expect us some time this morning."

"Taylor," Killian said, "You and I are going to have a word with Mr Sugden."

CHAPTER THIRTEEN

Peter Sugden lived opposite the pub in Polgarrow. Taylor shivered as they drove past Milly Lancaster's house and parked outside his bungalow.

He answered the door straight away. He was a rotund man with an extremely bulbous nose. From the blotches caused by burst blood vessels on his face, Taylor suspected he liked a drink or two.

"You must be the police," Sugden said to DI Killian. "Come in, but you'll have to excuse the mess. The cleaning girl only comes in on Wednesdays."

He led them inside to a musty-smelling living room. The stale smell of cigarette smoke lingered in the air.

"Take a seat." He pointed to a three-seater sofa. "Would you like some coffee?"

"No thanks," Killian said. "You phoned in to say you spoke to Milly Lancaster on Friday evening? Is that correct?"

"Terrible business. If I'd known what was going to happen, I'd have stopped her from getting in the car."

"What do you mean?" Taylor asked.

"You know. If I'd known she was about to drive off the cliff, of course I would've done something to stop her.

I couldn't believe it when I read the paper this morning. Do you mind if I smoke?"

Killian shook his head. Sugden took out a crumpled packet of Camel Plain, lit one and coughed.

"Terrible habit, I know," he said, "but after forty years, it's a bit late to stop now."

"Can you tell us about when you spoke to Milly Lancaster?" Killian said.

"It was Friday evening." Sugden inhaled deeply and blew out a cloud of smoke. "Around eight, I think. I always go to the Boar around that time. Four pints and I'm home by nine thirty. Milly was about to get into her car. She parks it by the pub — there's no space to park it by her house."

"What did you talk about?" Taylor asked.

"Nothing. I barely know Milly. Just enough to say hello, if you know what I mean."

"So you didn't speak to Mrs Lancaster?" Killian said.

"I just said hello, I made some comment about the weather and went inside the pub."

"How did Milly seem to you?" Taylor asked.

"What do you mean?"

"Did she appear anxious at all? Did she look like something was bothering her?"

"No, but then again, I'm not the most observant bloke in the world. My late wife, God rest her soul, used to moan like hell about it. Said I never noticed a thing. Milly seemed fine to me."

"So she got in her car," Killian said. "Did you see which direction she went in?"

"Up towards Bodgarth. It's on the way to Merryhead."

"I know where it is," Killian said.

"Did you see anybody else hanging around?" Taylor asked. "Did anybody follow Mrs Lancaster?"

"Not that I'm aware of, but, like I said, I don't notice much. I'm sorry I can't be of more help."

The room was now so full of smoke that Taylor's eyes were stinging.

"Thank you for your time, Mr Sugden," Killian said. "If you think of anything else, please phone me on my mobile." He handed Sugden one of his cards. "We'll see ourselves out," he added.

"Any use, do you think?" Taylor asked as they walked back to Killian's car.

"Might be, if something else turns up. Sugden might have given us something that just makes everything fall into place."

Taylor had worked with Killian for six months now and his optimism still amazed her. She had never come across somebody so positive about everything. She was about to get into the car when she spotted the curtains in Alice Green's house moving. "Sir, there's something I need to talk to Alice Green about. She's Milly's best friend." She pointed to Alice's house.

Alice was waiting for them at the front door. "Morning, love," she said to Taylor, eyeing Killian with obvious suspicion.

"Good morning, Mrs Green," Taylor said. "This is Detective Inspector Killian. Can we have a quick word?"

"Detective Inspector?" Alice seemed impressed. "Come in. It's not every day I have a police inspector in my house."

They went inside to the kitchen. The jackdaw cawed loudly when they sat down at the table.

"Please excuse him," Alice said. "He's got the manners of a pig sometimes."

"Jackdaws are amazing birds," said Killian. He looked at the bird. "I rescued one when I was a kid. Kept it for three years."

"Do you know Peter Sugden?" Taylor asked.

"Oh, I know Sugden very well. Real creep, that one. Thinks he's God's gift. I mean, have you seen the state of him?"

"What do you mean?"

"Uglier than a warthog in drag, he is. Just because he's got a bit of money, he thinks he's hot property. He took a fancy to poor Milly a while back."

"Did he now?" Killian said.

"He wouldn't leave her alone. He'd come calling day and night. Milly wasn't interested, but men like Sugden don't seem to get the hint."

"Men like Sugden?" Taylor repeated.

"Perverts, for want of a better word. I can tell you it was borderline stalking. He just wouldn't take no for an answer. Why are you so interested in Peter Sugden?"

"He claims he spoke to Milly the evening she disappeared," Killian said, "and he said he saw her drive off in the direction of Merryhead."

"And you believe him?"

"Why would he lie?" Taylor asked her.

"Milly never mentioned anything to me about going up to Merryhead. And Milly told me everything. Would you like a cup of tea?"

"No, thank you. We have to be going. We have a lot to get through today."

"It was lovely to see you again," Alice said to Taylor. "And it was nice to meet you, Detective Inspector."

CHAPTER FOURTEEN

"What did you make of that?" Taylor asked Killian as they drove back to Trotterdown.

"Somebody's lying to us," Killian said, "and I don't think it's the beekeeper. Peter Sugden said he hardly knew Milly Lancaster, but Alice Green told us a different story."

"Aren't we going to speak with Sugden again? There's something odd about him. Why phone in with information and then lie to us?" Taylor said.

"You know what it's like. People have all sorts of reasons for being cagey with the police. But yes, I've got my eye on Mr Sugden. He's hiding something. I can feel it," Killian replied.

"Why don't we go back?"

"Not yet. At this moment, Sugden believes he's done his civic duty and that's the end of it. I'm going to give it a few hours and wait until the pub opens. Then I'll send one of the Whites to check out Sugden's story. Did he really go to the pub that night or was he up on Merryhead too?"

A suspect at last, thought Taylor. Finally they were getting somewhere. They drove in silence the rest of the way to Trotterdown, where the newspaper reporters were still waiting round.

"DC Taylor!" A woman approached them. "Do you have any more information for us?"

Taylor wondered how she knew her name.

"DC Taylor?"

"No comment." Taylor pushed past her and followed Killian into the station, then to the canteen. DS Duncan was sitting at the same table with PC Eric White.

"Where've you been hiding?" Killian asked Duncan.

"Flu." Duncan sniffed. "I should be in bed."

"Flu in summer?" Taylor sat down next to Killian.

"Since most of us are here," Killian said, "we can go through what we have so far. Eric, I've got a job for you."

He filled Eric and Duncan in on the Sugden interview. "Do you think he killed Milly Lancaster?" White asked.

"We don't know yet. That's why I need you to check out his story. Sugden claims he spoke to Mrs Lancaster on Friday evening. He watched her drive off and then went inside the pub. It's the Old Boar in Polgarrow. They should be opening soon. I want you to find out if Sugden's story checks out. If it does, we're right back to square one."

"And if it doesn't?" Duncan said.

"Then we'll bring Sugden in. Apparently, he had a bit of a thing for Milly Lancaster a while ago."

"That's no reason to kill her." Duncan took out a handkerchief and blew his nose.

"Stranger things have happened. Maybe she spurned his advances and he got angry."

"I don't know," said Taylor, "something doesn't seem right. Sugden might be a bit weird, but I can't imagine him killing anybody."

"Maybe it was a spur of the moment thing," Eric suggested. "A crime of passion."

"Rubbish," Duncan said. "There's no such thing."

"For once I'm inclined to agree with DS Duncan," said Killian. "The evidence we have so far suggests this was planned. The doors in the car were jammed closed. You don't do that on the spur of the moment."

"So you're saying someone planned it beforehand and just waited for the right moment?" Eric asked.

"I don't know, but Sugden's all we have at the moment. We'll see if his story checks out and take it from there."

Duncan sneezed so hard that his knee shot up and hit the bottom of the table. "Go home," Killian told him. "You're no good to anybody in this state."

PC Thomas White came in and took Duncan's place, looking exhausted. "We've had over two hundred phone calls this morning."

"And?" Killian said.

"I've devised a system. A kind of sliding scale. The obvious time-wasters are at the bottom, followed by the probable attention-seekers. Then there are the maybes and the ones to definitely follow up are at the top. So far we have three people who might be able to help us."

"Only three?" Taylor asked. "Who are they?"

"There's Peter Sugden to start with."

"We're onto him already," Killian said. "Who are the other two?"

"A woman walking her dog thinks she saw a car like Milly Lancaster's up near Merryhead on Friday evening, and a hiker also claims to have seen the car up there. He walked straight past it and he thinks there were two people inside."

"Good. That's a start. Taylor, you can talk to the hiker and I'll leave it up to the Whites to decide between the dog walker and Peter Sugden."

"I'll take the pub in Polgarrow," Eric said.

"Let's get onto it, then. I'm going to keep our friends in the press up-to-date on what's going on."

"Why are you so friendly with them?" Taylor asked him.

"They're a necessary evil," Killian told her, "and whether we like it or not, they're not going anywhere."

CHAPTER FIFTEEN

Taylor parked outside the youth hostel in Trotterdown. She had never seen the attraction of youth hostels — sweaty student types cramped into tiny dormitories, swapping identical stories of "unique" travel experiences and thinking the world was theirs for the taking. She opened the door and approached the reception area. A young woman with blonde dreadlocks was staring at a computer screen behind the desk. She had piercings in her nose, ears and top lip.

"Morning," the girl said. She had an Australian accent. "Welcome to the Trotterdown Backpackers."

"I'm looking for Michael Newton. I believe he's staying here. Do you know where I can find him?" Taylor took out her ID and showed it to the woman.

"Mike? What's he done?"

"He phoned in with some information. I just need to ask him a few questions."

"Is this about the old woman?"

"Do you know where I can find him?" Taylor asked as politely as she could manage.

"He'll be in the courtyard. He sits there most of the day reading. It's out there." The woman pointed to a door to the right of the reception area.

Michael Newton was not at all what Taylor was expecting to find in a youth hostel. He was at least twice her age, balding with a thin pencil moustache. He was also wearing the thickest pair of glasses she had ever seen.

"Michael Newton?" Taylor said.

"Call me Mike. Dr Livingstone, I presume? Sorry, that's just my pathetic excuse for a joke. You must be from the police. Please take a seat."

Taylor sat opposite him on a stone bench. Mike set his book down on the table next to it. It was Tolstoy's *War and Peace.*

"Third time lucky," Mike told her. "I'm determined to get to the end this time. I don't know anybody who's ever managed to get to the end. Have you tried it?"

"No," said Taylor. "You called us this morning with some information about the car that went over the cliff at Merryhead."

"I couldn't believe it when I read about it. That poor old woman."

"What were you doing up on Merryhead on Friday evening?"

"Do I need a lawyer?" Mike's tone turned serious, but then his face broke into a wry smile. "I'm just kidding. I'm a lawyer myself. When I say that, I mean I'm qualified but I don't practise the dark art. I do a bit of lecturing when the need arises. Those that can't and all that. I was out hiking and I got a bit lost, I'm afraid. My sense of direction isn't exactly GPS standard. I was worried I might have to camp out for the night. Somehow I came across the road that leads down from Merryhead."

"What time was this?"

"It was starting to get dark. So around nine? I didn't get back here until after midnight."

"And you saw the car parked up there?"

"I didn't think much of it at the time. I just assumed it was a couple of young love-birds up there for the atmosphere."

"So there were two people in the car?"

"It was quite dark, but there were definitely two people in there. No mistake."

"Can you describe them?"

"Not really. Like I said, it was dark and I gave them a wide berth. I didn't think they'd appreciate being disturbed."

"Was it a man and a woman?"

"I think so, but they both had short hair. I'm certain of that."

"So you left Merryhead and walked all the way back to Trotterdown?"

"Yes. I didn't realise how long it was going to take."

"If you don't mind me asking," Taylor said, "isn't it a bit odd for a man like you to be staying in a place like this?"

"They're cheap, simple and I like the vibe in these places. All the best people are travellers. Look at Dr Livingstone, searching for the source of the Nile, eh?"

"Thank you for your time." Taylor stood up. "I'll let you get back to *War and Peace*."

"You should give it a go some time," Mike said.

"I doubt I'll ever have time."

* * *

Killian rang as she got in her car. "Where are you?" he asked.

"I've just finished at the Backpackers. The hiker didn't give us much to go on beyond the fact he reckons it was a man and a woman in Milly Lancaster's car that evening. He's a bit weird, but there doesn't seem to be any reason to doubt him."

"That is corroborated by what the woman walking the dog said. But Eric found out something interesting at the pub."

"What?"

"Nobody remembers seeing Sugden in the pub that night. It might not mean much — the barman was new and a lot of the people there were tourists — but White talked to some of the locals and none of them saw him either. Sugden's story is starting to sound a bit dodgy."

"What do we do now?"

"PC White is bringing Sugden in as we speak, and as DS Duncan is man down, I want you to sit in on the interview with me. It'll be good experience for you."

"I'm on my way."

CHAPTER SIXTEEN

Peter Sugden sat slumped in the chair in one of the two interview rooms at Trotterdown police station, opposite Killian and Taylor.

"Mr Sugden, are you sure you don't want a solicitor with you?" Killian said.

"I've done nothing wrong. Why the hell would I need one?" Sugden's eye twitched.

"Because it's your legal right."

"I haven't done anything wrong," Sugden repeated.

"Let's get started, then." Killian pressed the green button on the recording device. "Interview with Peter Sugden commenced 13:46. Present, DI Killian and DC Taylor. For the record, legal representation has been offered to Mr Sugden, but he has refused it. Mr Sugden, when we spoke to you earlier today you told us you spoke to Milly Lancaster last Friday evening. Is this correct?"

"Yes," Sugden scratched his twitching eye. "I mean, it could've been a bit earlier."

"What did you talk about?" Taylor asked.

"Not much. This and that. The weather. That kind of thing. Nothing important."

"Then what happened?" Killian said.

"She left. She drove off and I went to the pub."

"The Old Boar?"

"That's right."

"Did Mrs Lancaster say where she was going?" Taylor asked.

"No, and I didn't ask. It's none of my business. I've already told you all of this."

"We appreciate that," said Killian, "but we need it on the record."

"Can I smoke in here?"

"I'm afraid not. This is a non-smoking station. So Mrs Lancaster drove off and you went inside the pub? And this was around eight?"

"Round about. I had a few pints and then I left about nine thirty."

"Which direction did Mrs Lancaster go in?" Taylor asked.

"Up past the general store."

"In the direction of Merryhead, then?"

"I suppose so."

"So you stood and watched her drive up the road before entering the pub?"

"I don't know. I need a cigarette."

"We'll take a break in a minute," Killian said. "Did you speak to anybody in the pub? Somebody who might be able to corroborate your story?"

"I might have. I don't know. I think it was mostly tourists in there that night and there was a new barman working there. I hadn't seen him before."

"Boss," Taylor said to Killian, "can I have a word?"

"Very well," Killian said, "interview paused at 13:51." He paused the machine. "You can have a smoke outside. You've got ten minutes." Thomas White took Sugden out.

"What is it?" Killian said.

"I think he may be telling the truth," Taylor replied.

"What do you mean?"

"If there was a new barman in the Boar that night and the place was full of tourists, none of them would have noticed Sugden. He's hardly that memorable."

"You'll soon learn how things are in Cornwall. I know for a fact the pub wasn't just full of tourists. There'll have been locals in there too. Sugden's lived here for a long time. If he was in there, someone would have noticed. That man's not telling us everything. Let's see what he has to say about harassing Mrs Lancaster."

"Interview with Peter Sugden recommenced 14:10," Killian said when Sugden was brought back in. He looked more relaxed. The cigarette had obviously calmed his nerves a bit.

"You said earlier that you barely knew Mrs Lancaster," Killian started.

"That's right." Sugden nodded.

"How long have you lived in Polgarrow?" Taylor asked him.

"Coming up for thirty years. I was lucky enough to take very early retirement. What's that got to do with anything?"

"Milly Lancaster lived there for almost as long," said Killian. "She lived down the road from you, and yet you claim you hardly knew her."

"I knew her enough to say hello. Milly kept herself to herself. She didn't get out much. What's going on here? Surely you don't think I had something to do with what happened?"

"Do you own a car?" Taylor asked.

"No, I can't see the point. I stay around Polgarrow mostly and if I do need to go into Trotterdown, there's the bus. Not owning a car isn't against the law, is it? This is ridiculous." Sugden stood up. "I don't have to put up with this. I know my rights."

"Sit down please, Mr Sugden," Killian said.

Sugden did as he was told. His forehead was sweaty.

"Mr Sugden," Taylor said, "you claim not to have known Mrs Lancaster very well, but we have reason to believe you were pestering her for some time. Is this true?"

Sugden opened his mouth to say something but closed it again. "I was lonely," he admitted eventually. "It was nothing sinister. I just thought that seeing as though we were both on our own, it might be good for us. I'm not a monster."

"And how did Mrs Lancaster react?" Killian asked.

"The stuck-up cow wasn't interested."

"And you persisted in harassing her?" Taylor pushed the point.

"I didn't harass her. I'd call it perseverance. Women are like that, aren't they?"

"Like what, Mr Sugden?" Taylor glared at him.

"You know what I mean. They say no, but they want you to carry on. In my day we used to call it playing hard to get."

"How long did you pursue Mrs Lancaster?" Killian said.

"A couple of months. Not more than that. Where did you hear all this?"

"That's not important."

"It was that crazy beekeeper, wasn't it? That friend of Milly's. She's not right in the head, that one. Who the hell keeps a jackdaw for a pet?" His face was getting redder and redder. "I didn't push her over the cliff," he added, "and if I'm under arrest, I think it's time I phoned my lawyer."

"You're not under arrest," Killian told him. "For the time being, you're merely helping us with our enquiries. We will, of course, need your fingerprints and a sample of your DNA but in the meantime you're free to go. Interview concluded at 14:20."

He switched off the machine.

"Mr Sugden," Taylor had one last question, "how did you feel when Milly Lancaster rejected you? Were you angry?"

"That stuck-up cow. Always thought she was better than me. Well, look what happened to her. Who's better off now? And I'm sure you're both aware you won't be able to use what I just said as that machine's off. Like I said, I know my rights. I'll see myself out, if you don't mind."

CHAPTER SEVENTEEN

"What do you think?" Taylor asked Killian in the canteen.

"I think you need to work on your interview technique. You came across as rather aggressive in there."

"Aggressive?" Taylor had left the interview room feeling quite pleased with herself. She thought she had done a good job.

"I don't like the man much myself," Killian said, "but there are ways to conduct an interview. You mustn't let personal feelings get in the way."

Taylor scowled.

"Don't look so hard done by," Killian added. "It was just an observation. I remember one of my first interviews. I got so frustrated with the suspect I ended up shouting at him that everyone knew he'd done it."

"Do you think Sugden was involved?"

"It's hard to tell. What do you think?"

"I don't know. If he was, he's a pretty good liar."

"Well, right now all we've got is a pub full of people who don't remember seeing Sugden there on Friday night, and the fact that he once made a play for the dead woman. Neither of which is enough to charge him with anything.

We'll have to wait and see if forensics can tie him to Milly Lancaster's car."

"So we just leave him alone?"

"We do the opposite. We'll keep an even closer eye on him. If he's hiding something, he's bound to slip up sooner or later. They always do."

"I wonder what went through her mind when she went over the cliff."

"Don't go there. Don't even think about it. Our job is to figure out what happened in the hours before that happened."

"Do you think her body will ever be found?"

"I doubt it. The tide will have taken her right out and ocean life will have done the rest."

Taylor shivered. What a terrible way to end up, she thought.

A huge raindrop hit the window, breaking her horrid thoughts. It was followed by another and then the heavens opened up.

"Summer rain shower," Killian said. "It'll all be over in an hour. Let's get going, anyway."

"Where are we going?"

"It's been an hour since we let Sugden go, so let's do something useful while we wait to see what forensics can come up with. We'll go and find out what makes Peter Sugden tick."

* * *

The Old Boar was surprisingly full for a Tuesday afternoon. An equal number of tourists and locals were eating at tables or drinking at the bar. Killian propelled Harriet towards a man in his sixties having a pint in the corner by the bar.

"Dennis Albarn," he whispered. "We're in luck. Dennis and Peter Sugden go way back." He sat down next to Albarn. "Dennis, can we have a word?"

Albarn shrugged. "Talk away," he said. He looked Taylor up and down and smiled. "Things are definitely looking up. In my day, police women were all big hips and hairy legs."

"Dennis and I are old acquaintances," Killian said, "and I'm sure this won't be the last time you meet him on your travels either."

"I did my time." Albarn looked at Harriet. "And I'm a changed man. What can I help you with? A drink, perhaps?"

"No thanks," Taylor said. "We'd actually like to speak to you about Peter Sugden."

"Scottish accent as well. It just gets better and better. What's old Sugden done? Exposed himself to the dinner ladies at the school?"

"Excuse me?"

"It was a joke, love. Relax. Sugden's a bit of a seed that's all."

"A seed?"

"Seedy. A bit of a perv, if you know what I mean. Everybody knows he's harmless really. Hasn't got it in him."

"So you know Mr Sugden quite well?"

"Not that well." Albarn finished the beer in his glass. "We exchange a few words when we're in here. We both like the horses. What's he done?"

"Nothing we're aware of," Killian said. "Were you in here last Friday night?"

"Probably." Albarn frowned. He was lost in thought for a moment. "The old memory's not what it was. I'll have to check my diary for you."

"This is serious," Killian said. "Think."

"Is this about Milly? What a terrible thing to happen."

"Did you know Mrs Lancaster?" Taylor asked him.

"For over forty years. She was Alice's best friend. I was the best man at Stanley and Alice's wedding."

"Were you in here on Friday night or not?" Killian sounded impatient.

"Guilty as charged," Albarn said. "I'm in here most nights. I'm retired now. It's not against the law, is it?"

"No, it isn't. Can you remember if Peter Sugden was here?"

"Not as far as I can remember." Albarn leaned across the bar.

"Another pint," he said to the barman.

"Are you sure?" Killian said.

"Sugden wasn't here." Albarn handed the barman a five pound note. "The place was full of tourists, mostly. Poncey types asking for craft beers and mojitos and what-have-you."

"What time were you here?" Taylor asked.

"Around six. I left about nine. I was supposed to meet Stan but he never showed up."

"Stanley Green?" Taylor was surprised. "Alice's husband? I thought he didn't live here anymore."

"He doesn't, but he visits from time to time. I bumped into him in Trotterdown last Wednesday. He's been living in Spain for a few years. Lucky bugger."

"So Sugden definitely didn't come in last Friday night?" Killian repeated.

"No. Why are you so interested in old Sugden?"

"Just curious," Killian said. "Thank you for your help."

"You know me, Jack. Always happy to help the police."

CHAPTER EIGHTEEN

The sun and the moon were in the sky together for a brief moment and then the sun disappeared behind the distant sea. The wind had picked up and the hollyhock bushes in Alice Green's back garden were swaying in the cool breeze. She looked over the hedge into the Sedgwicks' garden. The lights were on in the house, but Alice knew Eddie and Barbara were not at home. Eddie had told her they were going to watch a film in Trotterdown. She knew they would be gone for a good few hours but she still wanted to get what she was about to do over with as quickly as possible.

She got to work with her green shovel, digging up the soil under the hollyhocks. She carefully removed the earth around her husband's body, making sure not to dig too close to the corpse. It was hard work. After twenty minutes, Alice had only managed to dig a small hole. She wiped the sweat from her brow and carried on.

Two hours later, Stanley's body was lying on the grass. Alice had managed to drag him from under the bushes, but it had used up most of her energy. She looked at the dead body of the man she had married forty years ago. The skin on his face was grey in the moonlight. One of his eyes was missing. Where his ring finger had been was now just a black stump.

It had taken a huge amount of effort to drag the body the few metres from the bushes, and there was no way she was going to be able to get him to the road to where she'd parked her van. There was only one thing for it, even though the very idea made her want to vomit. She was running out of time and she couldn't leave the body lying on her back lawn. She went to the shed and grabbed her wheelbarrow and two industrial-strength refuse bags.

The moon vanished behind a large cloud and Alice could barely see what she was doing. She waited for her eyes to adjust to the darkness. The wind pushed the clouds away and the moon reappeared, lighting up Stanley's face. Alice wondered what had happened to his eye. It was odd seeing him so dirty. Stanley had always been neat and smartly dressed. It was one of the things she liked about him.

Alice put the shovel on the spot where the shirt and trousers met and suddenly thought of the day Stanley had come home wearing that shirt, over ten years ago. She'd told him it made him look like a man in the grip of a midlife crisis, but Stanley hadn't cared. He wore the shirt for years afterwards.

Alice closed her eyes and brought the shovel down with all her strength. The shovel didn't make any headway — the edge wasn't sharp enough. Alice started to panic. *What now?* She lifted the shovel up and examined it closely. *Why not?* She went into the house and returned with the whetstone she used to sharpen her kitchen knives.

Twenty minutes later, the shovel was ready. The sharpened edge glinted in the moonlight. Alice raised it up in the air, took a deep breath and brought it down with everything she had. There was a sickening crunch as the sharp edge of the shovel sliced through Stanley's pelvis and wedged in the grass underneath. She managed to prise the shovel loose and moved it into position for another go.

She paused for a moment to give herself a breather and thought about life with Stanley Green.

It hadn't always been bad. The first few years had been pretty good, in fact. Stanley was the perfect gentleman and he'd treated her like a princess. Then Alice thought about the first time she'd found out she was not the only princess in Stanley's life and brought the shovel down so hard it nearly sliced his body in half.

Emily Bright, Alice thought, that was her name. A most inappropriate name. Legs that went on forever and a brain whose only purpose was to fill in the gap between her ears. Emily Bright had been the first. Alice had lost count of exactly how many others had followed.

She lifted the shovel high in the air and slammed it down with all her might. Stanley Green's body separated into two parts, like an earthworm cut in half.

Alice wrapped the legs up first, put them in one of the refuse sacks and tied the opening with duct tape. She lifted the sack into the wheelbarrow and trundled it down towards her van. The road was deserted as she opened the back and bundled her husband's legs inside. It made her feel sick, but she went through the same thing with the other half of Stanley.

Driving the few miles up to Merryhead, Alice realised she was shaking. She could barely keep hold of the steering wheel. She slowed down and stopped by the side of the road. All sorts of memories were flooding her brain. Not just Stanley. Not just Emily and all the other little idiots who'd followed her. Other things she'd rather forget. Other things she had forgotten, till now.

There was quite a lot she remembered, if she put her mind to it. She stopped the car for a moment and wound down the window. She breathed in the night air and closed her eyes for a moment.

Get a hold on yourself, she thought. *So what if there are things you'd rather not have done? Sometimes you just have to do what's necessary. It's almost over, anyway. Everything can go back to normal soon. Or as normal as possible, anyway.*

She carried on towards the top of the cliff and parked as close to the edge as she dared. She got out of the van. The wind was now howling over the cliff top. She shivered. She could hear the sound of the waves crashing on the rocks below. She was in luck — the tide was in. If she acted quickly enough, the tide would carry Stanley's body parts far out to sea, never to be seen again. She opened up the van and looked around. Nothing and no one to be seen.

She emptied Stanley's legs onto on the grass with a dull thump and rolled them over the edge. She heard a splash as they hit the water. She sent the refuse sack after them and watched as it floated up in the wind and disappeared from view. The body was harder, because she had tied the tape on the sack too tightly. She could not risk throwing the body over inside the sack — it might float. She needed to get it out. With a desperate wrench, she managed to tear the tape and Stanley's body tumbled out. Alice closed her eyes and pushed it over the edge to be reunited with its legs. She almost screamed when the now empty refuse sack was picked up by the wind and carried out to sea.

As she drove back to Polgarrow, Alice's heartbeat slowly returned to normal. It was all over. Everything was going to be all right. She could go home and forget about Stanley forever. It would not be too difficult — after all, in the forty years they had been married, they had only really spent a few good years together. Alice was looking forward to a huge glass of port and a good night's sleep. Everything would be different in the morning. And if she did remember the other things too — well, she could deal with those in due course.

CHAPTER NINETEEN

Harriet Taylor woke up from a dream that she instantly forgot. She had a throbbing headache. Her stomach started to contract and she shot up, threw the duvet to the floor and made it to the bathroom just in time. She vomited into the sink.

She retched until she was certain there was nothing left in her stomach. She rinsed her mouth, splashed some cold water on her face and looked at her reflection in the mirror. She was shocked at what she saw. Her face was pale and her green eyes were bloodshot.

Harriet went downstairs and looked at the kettle. She was not sure if her stomach could even handle a cup of peppermint tea, but she decided to risk it and turned the kettle on. She spotted the empty wine bottle on the kitchen table and got flashbacks of the previous night. A whole bottle of white wine and two sleeping pills had ensured a good night's sleep but the consequences were evident in the bathroom sink.

"Never again," she said.

She felt terrible. Her headache was getting worse and her stomach was making strange gurgling noises. She sipped her tea and it calmed her stomach a little. *What made me drink a bottle of wine after all this time?* "Never again," she repeated, gulping two painkillers with more tea.

She opened the back door and a cool breeze wafted in. She took a big gulp of air. The painkillers were starting to work and the peppermint tea had settled her stomach a bit. She scowled at the empty bottle of wine and threw it in the recycling. The wine had stood untouched in the fridge for months.

What made me open it last night?

Then she remembered. Yesterday would have been Danny's birthday. Charming, two-timing Danny Taylor would have been thirty years old. Taylor had thought a lot about how life would have been if Danny hadn't been killed in the accident. She wondered how much longer he would have taken her for a fool.

The truth was that the wine hadn't been to drown her sorrows. It had been to celebrate the fact that he had died and spared her further humiliation. Danny's death that night had hit her hard at the time, but, in fact, losing him had given her some semblance of a life again. She forced down the rest of the tea and went upstairs for a shower. A cold one, as cold as she could tolerate.

* * *

A few miles away, Alice Green woke with a smile on her face. She wasn't sure why. Was it the result of a dream? She couldn't remember. All she knew was that it was all over. Stanley was gone for good and she would never have to worry about him again. As she walked through to the kitchen in her nightdress, she noticed that the smile would not shift. It felt like a mask glued to her face.

"Cup of tea?" The jackdaw cawed as Alice turned on the kettle. "Cup of tea?"

"Clever boy." Alice opened a fresh tin of dog food and emptied some of it into the tray at the bottom of the cage. "It's a beautiful day, my boy. The bees are going to be in their element today."

She opened the window as the kettle boiled. The scent of the hollyhocks drifted into the kitchen. She looked outside and her smile disappeared abruptly. There was a gaping trench under the hollyhock bushes and a huge pile of soil on the grass next to them. In her haste to get rid of the body, Alice had forgotten to fill in the hole. She ran outside still in her nightdress and grabbed the shovel still lying on the grass.

"Oh dear." Eddie Sedgwick's head appeared above the hedge that divided the two gardens. "Looks like you had a visit from a badger last night. A big one, by the look of things. I wonder what it was looking for."

Alice had to think quickly. "Probably scouting for somewhere to spend the winter," she said.

"Do you need some help? I'm pretty handy with a spade, even though I do say so myself."

"No thanks, Eddie." Alice began shovelling the loose earth into the hole. "It shouldn't take long."

"Lovely day for it, anyway," Eddie said and went back inside.

Just bugger off, you nosy bastard, Alice thought, but she managed to bite her tongue.

Twenty minutes later, she was finished. She trampled on the last of the soil and stood back to admire her work. It was as if nothing had ever happened. Some soil was still scattered on the grass, but a good downpour would clear that up. Alice went back inside for a well-earned cup of tea.

"Stanley Green," she raised the teacup in the air, "good riddance."

She was free of him now. He would no longer haunt her. She wondered where he'd ended up.

Miles out to sea, never to be seen again.

CHAPTER TWENTY

Harriet Taylor was about to leave for work when someone knocked at her front door. She opened it and saw DI Jack Killian standing in the doorway, wearing a very grave expression.

"Sir?" Taylor asked. "What's wrong?"

"I'm glad I caught you," Killian said. "Are you all right? You don't look too well."

"I'm fine," she lied. "Did forensics find something?"

"I'm afraid this is about something else entirely. The Milly Lancaster investigation is going to have to be put on hold."

"Sounds serious."

"Let's get going, then."

"Where are we going?"

"Down to the harbour. And I sincerely hope you're not the squeamish type."

* * *

As they drove towards the harbour entrance, Killian told Taylor how someone had rung the station in the early hours of that morning.

"A fishing boat dragged something up in its net," he said, "and when the net was emptied on the deck, the skipper almost fainted. It was a human body."

Taylor flinched. "Milly Lancaster?"

"It's the body of a man. And when I say body, I mean it literally. The legs are missing."

The nausea from earlier that morning hit Taylor's stomach again.

"He's been cut in half," Killian continued. "The skipper of the boat thinks it may have been a shark attack."

"A shark?" It sounded unbelievable.

"We do get shark attacks round here every so often."

"What kind of a shark can bite a man in half?"

"Not many. And you hardly ever get that type in these waters."

Killian stopped the car by the harbour breakwater. The sheltered marina was abuzz with people. Gulls swarmed overhead. Every now and then, one swooped down to retrieve something from the water.

"It's worse than I expected," said Killian. "I thought it might be busy at this time of year, but a shark attack around here is going to cause panic."

"What do we do?"

"Damage control, for what it's worth. We're probably already too late. Word travels quickly in this place."

He headed towards the wharf where the fishing boats were usually tied up. It was obvious which one had pulled the body up in its nets. A crowd of people had gathered on the wharf next to a blue-and-white boat with the name 'Serenity' on the side. Two policemen in uniform were trying to keep the hoard away from it. They seemed to be fighting a losing battle. As they got closer, Taylor saw it was the PCs Eric and Thomas White.

"Morning," Killian said to Eric. "Where's the body?"

"Still on the boat, sir. The skipper had the good sense to cover it with a tarpaulin. There's an ambulance on its way now."

"Good."

"Where's the captain of the boat?" Taylor asked.

"Inside the wheelhouse. He's in a bit of a state," Eric said.

"Get these rubberneckers out of here." Killian pointed to the people gawping at the boat. "I want this whole wharf cleared by the time the ambulance gets here."

Eric and Thomas set about dispersing the crowds and Killian stepped aboard the boat. The way he skipped from the wharf onto the deck made Taylor think it wasn't the first time he'd done it. "Come on," he called.

She leaned over and grabbed the safety rail so tightly that her knuckles turned white, before she managed to scramble on board. Serenity was an old-fashioned trawler with a centre cabin. The tarpaulin she'd heard about lay on the deck at the stern and the boat's skipper was sipping coffee in the wheelhouse. The stench of rotten fish and diesel didn't help Taylor's delicate stomach.

The captain looked more like a schoolteacher than a sailor. He was slim with thinning hair and rimless spectacles. Only the badly-fitting oilskins identified him as a fisherman.

"You must be the police," he said. "I'm Gary. Gary Dean. This is my boat."

"Mr Dean, I'm DI Killian and this is DC Taylor. We need to ask you a few questions."

"Of course." Dean put his coffee cup down on the steering console. His hands were shaking badly.

"I covered the body up," he said. "I couldn't bear to look at it."

"It's all right, Mr Dean," Taylor told him. "There's an ambulance on the way to take it away."

"Have you seen it? Don't look at it. I can't get it out of my head. I don't think I'll ever get it out of my head." He looked terrified and sick at the same time.

"What time did you discover it?" Killian came straight to the point.

"It was around six this morning."

"Where was this?"

"About ten nautical miles out, pretty much as the crow flies, from the harbour."

"What were you doing out so early?" Taylor said.

Dean looked at her as though she had asked him why his eyes were blue. "I cast off around midnight. At this time of year the best fishing is before dawn."

"What do you fish for? I thought trawling was illegal." She'd read an article about the issue in the local paper, and was rather proud that she knew the correct terminology.

"It is. The size of the nets is regulated. I don't really trawl. Not in the traditional or commercial sense. I just catch enough to sell at the markets. I supply some of the restaurants in town too."

"So you found the body around six," Killian said, "then what?"

"Then what?" Dean giggled nervously. "I screamed, that's what. I screamed my bloody head off. I almost threw the body back where it came from."

"I'm glad you didn't."

"Then I turned the boat round and came back here as fast as the engine would let me. I got back at around seven and phoned you lot."

"How long have you been fishing these waters?" Taylor asked.

"Over twenty years. I used to fish with my dad and now he's gone, the boat's mine. I'm thinking of selling her after this."

"Twenty years." Taylor was genuinely interested. "How many sharks have you seen in that time?"

"Quite a few. They get caught up in the nets sometimes. But they're just small ones. Two or three feet."

"Nothing bigger than that?"

"You don't see the bigger sharks. They certainly see you though."

"So you haven't seen any sharks that could do that to a man?" She pointed to the tarpaulin on the deck.

"Bloody hell, no. You've seen the film *Jaws*, haven't you? That's the only shark I can think of that could do this."

"Are you ready?" Killian asked Taylor. He nodded to the tarpaulin.

"If it's all right with you," said Dean, "I'd rather not go with you. I'll stay up here."

"Of course," Killian nodded again and stepped down to the deck. The tarpaulin lay next to a crate full of fish. Most of them were dead but a few were flipping around in a desperate attempt to cling to life. "Here goes." He took hold of the tarpaulin.

Taylor wasn't sure how she was going to react. She had seen dead bodies before, but they'd still had their legs attached. *Please don't faint in front of the DI*, she told herself.

In fact, the body did not even look like a body. It was more like a checked shirt with a blue head and two blue hands. Taylor stared at the face. It was slightly bloated and one of the eyes was missing. Thin grey hair sprouted in patches from the dead man's head.

"My God." Killian turned away.

Taylor just stared. The hands were shrivelled. One of the fingers was missing. The lips and eyelids were a lighter shade of blue than the rest of the face. She took in everything, starting from the top of the head and continuing to where the shirt ended and the legs ought to have been.

"Seen enough?" Killian looked as though he was going to be sick.

"Yes." Taylor replaced the tarpaulin. "Enough to know this wasn't a shark attack."

CHAPTER TWENTY-ONE

Taylor watched as two paramedics put the body in a bag, hauled it onto the wharf and placed it on a stretcher. She followed them to the ambulance parked at the end of the pier. Jack Killian walked after her. He looked queasy.

"Jack," the older of the paramedics said, "do you want us to check you over? You don't look too great, my friend."

"I'm fine," Killian said gruffly. "What now?"

The paramedic looked at the body bag on the stretcher and then back at Killian.

"We're good, Jack," he smiled, "but we're not that good. I don't think this one's going to make it."

Taylor started to laugh, slightly hysterically. Killian cast her a stern glance and she tried to stifle it.

"Where are you taking him?" he asked.

"Back to the mortuary."

"Here or Plymouth?"

"We'll keep him in town. I'm sure you're curious as to what happened to old Arthur here."

"Arthur?" Taylor broke in. "Do you know who it is?"

"It's his sick attempt at humour," Killian told her. "Meet Carl Morton. Veteran paramedic and terrible stand-up comedian."

"Let's go," Morton said to his colleague. They wheeled the stretcher into the ambulance, jumped in behind it and closed the doors. It drove off at a leisurely pace.

"Quite a character, that one," Taylor said.

"Carl? An acquired taste, I can tell you that."

"Why did he call the body Arthur?"

"You'll figure it out. What did you mean back there when you said this wasn't a shark attack?"

"I've watched the odd documentary on sharks. Did you know that they don't actually like the taste of humans? They usually bite and let go. Unfortunately, that's sometimes enough to kill you."

"I'm ignoring your liking for nature documentaries. I suppose it's better than those awful so-called police dramas. Go on."

"One bite from a shark would have ripped that body to pieces. They've got serrated teeth — each tooth has rows of much smaller teeth. But the shirt on that body was hardly torn. It can't have been a shark, even a massive *Jaws*-style one."

"Interesting. We'll see what the path guys have to say."

"And how did he get in the water in the first place?"

"I don't know. Maybe he went for a midnight dip?"

"In a checked shirt? No, I don't buy it. Something else happened to him."

Killian sighed. "Be that as it may, for the time being we keep to the story of a shark attack."

"Damage control?"

"Precisely. Better to let the public believe a shark did it than have them coming up with all kinds of wonderful theories."

On the way back to Killian's car, Taylor's vision went black for a few seconds and she had to steady herself on the railing of the jetty.

"Are you all right?" Killian asked. Taylor could see his lips move but the words seemed to come out in slow motion.

"Taylor?" Killian looked very concerned now.

Taylor felt extremely cold. Her legs were numb. She sat down on the concrete of the wharf and leaned against the railing. She tried to concentrate on one of the boats in the harbour, a large pleasure craft with 'Kittiwake' on the hull and a family of gulls sitting on the bow. She took a few deep breaths and the feeling slowly started to come back to her legs.

"Harriet?" Killian was leaning over her. He never used her first name.

"I'm all right," she said, "I think the shock of seeing that body is catching up with me."

She knew this wasn't true. The sight of the severed torso had hardly troubled her. The numbness was the after-effect of the combination of an entire bottle of wine and the sleeping tablets. Taylor promised herself never to mix the two again.

"Help me up." She reached her hand out to Killian. The DI pulled her to her feet, but he still looked extremely concerned.

"I'm fine," Taylor insisted. "We've got work to do."

On the way back to the station, Taylor gazed out of the window and thought about the body. She could not think of a plausible explanation as to why he'd ended up in a fishing boat's nets. It didn't make any sense.

"How do you think he ended up in the sea?" Killian asked. He was clearly thinking the same thing.

"I can't imagine. Do you think we'll be able to find out who he is?"

"That depends. The pathology guys will be able to tell roughly when he died. If he was in the water for some time, it'll be a bit harder to get a precise time of death though."

"Somebody must know who he is. Surely somebody will be missing him."

"Not necessarily."

"What about missing persons?"

"We don't even know if he's from around here. It'll take forever to check the database for the whole country and if he's a foreigner, it'll be almost impossible to find out who he is."

"First an old lady gets pushed over the cliff in her car and then an old man ends up in the nets of a fishing boat. Do you think the two are connected?"

"Not at the moment. As far as I'm concerned, it's just a coincidence." He turned the car right and headed inland.

"Where are you going? The station's in the other direction."

"Slight change of plan. I'm getting tired of twiddling my thumbs waiting to see what forensics can come up with. Those guys tend to work much quicker when they have someone breathing down their necks. I want to know if our friend Peter Sugden can be linked in any way to Milly Lancaster's car."

CHAPTER TWENTY-TWO

Alice carefully removed the frame from the hive and examined it closely. She'd made sure to wear gloves this time. When she'd first started beekeeping, she used to wear a full protective suit and hood, but over time she'd realised that her nice Italian bees made this unnecessary. Also the bees got used to you, in a way. But the bees had hardly produced any honey since the last time she'd checked. She couldn't understand what the problem was, after they'd been performing so beautifully for the past month. She shrugged and slid the frame back into position.

Maybe I need to buy more hives.

She looked around the garden. There was plenty of space for a few more hives and she could always plant some more hollyhock bushes. The bees seemed to like the hollyhocks best.

Alice made a cup of tea and sat down at the kitchen table. There was a letter she needed to write. Stanley had a sister, Rita, in Canada who Alice wrote to every month. Rita had tried to persuade Alice to buy a computer and get Skype, but Alice wasn't going to start messing with things like that at her age.

There was a lot of news this month. Alice began with the tragic death of her old friend Milly. She explained that the police didn't know what had happened but that she was sure they would get to the bottom of it. She didn't mention Stanley's demise.

She looked in the kitchen drawer for a stamp and remembered she'd used the last one on the previous letter. She sighed and picked up her handbag. She would have to go to the village post office.

The sun on her face made her smile. June was definitely the best time of the year in Cornwall. She walked past where Milly used to park her car and intense sadness hit her. Milly had been her only real friend and she was gone.

A police car was parked outside Peter Sugden's house. Alice had never liked Sugden. And he'd been after Milly. Nasty piece of work.

The police car was still there as she came back from the post office. Alice slowed down and tried to peer into Sugden's house. She could see two policemen in uniform. They were opening cupboards and drawers in the living room, looking for something. She looked at her watch. Half past twelve.

She went into the Old Boar. "Small port, love," she said to the young barman and took it to the window, where she could get a good view of Peter Sugden's house. After a few minutes, the two policemen came out with Sugden. He didn't look pleased at all. Alice watched as he locked his front door and got in the back of the police car.

CHAPTER TWENTY-THREE

Taylor, Killian and DS Duncan sat in the station canteen. Peter Sugden was in one of the holding cells next to the interview rooms. They were waiting for Sugden's solicitor to arrive from Plymouth. The forensics people had stumbled upon something interesting, though more by chance than anything else.

Inside the lock on the passenger side of Milly Lancaster's car, they had found some small slivers of a different metal: a mix of nickel and chromium. Alan Littlemore, the head of forensics, was of the opinion that the metal came from some kind of tool — a screwdriver maybe — which had been used to jam the lock. PCs White and White had been granted permission to search Peter Sugden's house and Eric White had discovered a screwdriver made of the same metal in the wheelie bin in his back garden. It was still in working order, apart from some slight wear on the tip, and it was now in the hands of the forensics department.

"Looks like we've got the bastard." Duncan looked smug. "I've known old Sugden for years. I knew there was something not quite right about him."

"Don't get too excited," Killian said, "let's see what forensics have to say first. It may be a different screwdriver."

"Come on, Jack, there was bugger-all wrong with it. Why would he throw it away unless he wanted rid of the evidence? It was an expensive one, too. No, Sugden's our man."

"I still don't see the motive," Taylor said. "Sugden's a bit odd, but that doesn't make him a killer. We need more proof, not just some chucked-out tool. When is his solicitor getting here?"

"He'll be an hour or so," Killian told her. "He's still in court."

"He can take his time," said Duncan. "Let Sugden stew in the cell for a bit. It'll do us good. Who's he got?"

"Justin Stanford. I've never met him."

"I have," Duncan said. "Real smarmy git. Makes a living getting scumbags off the hook."

Thomas White walked in. "Sorry to disturb you sir," he said to Killian, "but I thought you'd want to know that forensics have matched the metal found in the car lock to the screwdriver."

"Are they a hundred percent sure?"

"Do you want to ask Littlemore if he's a hundred percent sure?"

"That's that, then." Killian stood up. "In the years I've known Littlemore, the man has never been wrong about anything in his field. Let's get a cup of coffee while we wait for Sugden's solicitor. I've a feeling we're in for a rough few days."

Taylor gazed out of the window. She could just make out the blue of the Atlantic in the distance. She sipped another cup of peppermint tea. Her stomach felt much better now and the dizziness was gone.

"I want to talk to that scumbag." Duncan slurped a mouthful of coffee. "You and me. Jack. It'll be just like the old days."

"I've been thinking about that," Killian said. "Taylor and I did the initial interview, and it went quite well. I think it would be better if she interviewed Sugden with me. For the sake of consistency, I mean."

"Seriously, Jack? Her?" Duncan glared at Taylor. "What does she know about interrogating a murderer?"

"Suspected murderer. And she's more than up to the job." Killian smiled at her. "Try not to be so aggressive this time, though," he added. "Sugden's solicitor will cut you down in an instant."

"I can do nice," Taylor said. "I'll just follow your lead and watch Sugden like a hawk. How d'you want to play it?"

"This is nonsense," Duncan said. "I'm the experienced one here." He kicked his chair for effect and walked out of the canteen.

"Ignore him," Killian told her. "It's just sour grapes. Anyway, to answer your question, I'm not sure. I'm still not sure about him either."

"What do you mean?"

"I can't figure out why he'd want to kill Milly Lancaster. It doesn't make any sense."

"What about the evidence?"

"We don't have enough yet. And there's no inkling of a motive."

"Crime of passion?" she suggested.

"Maybe." Killian sounded unconvinced.

CHAPTER TWENTY-FOUR

Peter Sugden's solicitor arrived two hours later. After a brief consultation with his client in the holding cell, he, Sugden, Killian and Taylor gathered in interview room two. Killian turned on the recording device.

"Interview with Peter Sugden," he said, "Present, DI Killian, DC Taylor and Justin Stanford."

"Detective Inspector," Stanford broke in, "before we begin, I have to inform you I have instructed my client not to say anything."

"I thought you might."

"My client claims he knows nothing about what he is being accused of, and to be honest, I find these allegations absurd. Mr Sugden has never been in trouble with the law before and I suggest you rethink the consequences of this outrageous charge."

"I'd say that's all the more reason for your client to talk to us, so we can eliminate him from our enquiries."

"Detective, I'm sure you're aware of the law. There's a little part of it about being innocent until proven guilty."

The smug smile on Stanford's face was making Taylor's blood boil. She took a deep breath.

"Mr Stanford," Killian said, "whether your client is innocent or guilty is neither here nor there at the moment. We have enough evidence to charge him and whether he decides to speak to us or not, we have the power to hold him for forty-eight hours."

"Is that right?" Sugden suddenly found his tongue. "Can they lock me up for two days?"

"You don't have to say anything," Stanford told him.

"I haven't done anything. I want to go home."

"Mr Sugden," Stanford said, "I know what I'm doing. You have the right not to say anything, and I advise you strongly to make full use of that right." He took out his phone and looked at the screen.

"I didn't kill Milly Lancaster," Sugden said. "I liked Milly. Why would I want to kill her?"

"That's not what you said the last time we spoke," Taylor reminded him. "I think the exact words you used were 'stuck-up cow.'"

"That doesn't mean I wanted to kill her."

"OK," Killian said, "now we're all on the same page, how do you explain the screwdriver we found in your wheelie bin?"

"I don't know. It's not mine. Anybody could have put it in there."

"Why would anybody do that?" Taylor said.

"I don't know. I can't believe this is happening," Sugden protested.

"Are you saying somebody crept into your back garden and dumped the screwdriver in the wheelie bin?"

"Constable," Stanford shook his head, "please stop putting words in my client's mouth."

"I'm not putting words in his mouth. It was a simple question."

"OK." Killian took charge. "A while ago you made certain advances towards Mrs Lancaster. She turned you down. You also claimed that you were in the Old Boar last Friday night. We have a witness, a man who knows you very well, in fact, and he's positive you weren't in the pub that night."

"Who's that, then?"

"And now we find a screwdriver in your bin. A screwdriver that can be linked to the locks on Milly Lancaster's car door. How do you explain all of this, Mr Sugden? There are far too many coincidences here."

"I don't know." Sugden looked like he was going to burst into tears. "I didn't kill her. I didn't kill Milly."

"I suggest we take a short break," Stanford broke in. "I need to speak with my client in private."

"I'm not finished yet," Killian replied. "Why did you lie about being in the pub last Friday?"

"I was scared. I panicked."

"That's enough," Stanford said.

"Go on," Taylor said.

"When you lot came around, I got scared. I didn't think anybody would remember me not being in the pub. I didn't expect all this to happen."

"What else have you lied about?" Taylor said.

"That's enough," Stanford repeated. "A short break is in order and if you persist in badgering my client, there'll be hell to pay."

Taylor looked to Killian for support. He sighed and gave a slight shake of his head. "I think we're done here anyway," he announced. "Interview with Peter Sugden concluded."

"I'm sorry," Taylor said to Killian after Sugden and his solicitor had left the room.

"Don't be. That went better than I expected."

"I wasn't too aggressive?"

"Why do you think I chose you over Duncan? No, you did well back there. We've got Sugden crapping in his pants, if you'll excuse my language. They tend to slip up more when they've been shaken a bit."

"Do you think he did it?"

"I think we need to do a bit of digging around in Peter Sugden's life. Let's see what kind of skeletons we find."

CHAPTER TWENTY-FIVE

Harriet Taylor knocked on the door and waited. DI Killian had been called away on a family emergency. His wife had been rushed to hospital, he told her before dashing out to the car park.

Alice Green opened the door. "Hello, my dear," she said, smiling, "come in. I've just made a fresh pot of tea." Taylor followed her inside.

"Hello," the jackdaw squawked, "hello."

"How many words does he know?" Taylor asked.

"Too many. I have to be careful what I say in front of him. Would you like some tea? And a piece of bread and honey? I'm still a little concerned about it, but really I'm sure it's fine." Alice poured two cups of tea from an old teapot and opened a jar. "You need more flesh on your bones. Is this about Milly? Have you found something?"

"We still haven't found her body, but we have arrested somebody in connection with Milly's disappearance. That's why I'm here. We're speaking to everybody who knows Peter Sugden."

"You've arrested Sugden?" Alice took a sip of tea and grinned.

"I can't go into the details, but a number of things point in his direction. Too many for us to ignore, I'm afraid. I know you don't particularly like the man, but what else can you tell us about him?"

"He's slightly odd," Alice said. "I mean, there's something definitely not quite right about him, if you know what I mean."

"I'm afraid I don't."

"It's as if he carries this presence around with him, like a negative aura. It's hard to define. Most people don't feel it, but I've seen dogs growl at him for no reason. Children cross the street when they see him coming."

"I see." Taylor nibbled a piece of bread and honey. It tasted fine to her.

"You say you have some evidence? Some things that point in his direction?"

"Like I said, I'm not at liberty to discuss that. Evidence is all very well but what we can't seem to fathom out is why anybody would want to kill Milly in the first place. It doesn't make any sense."

"I can't understand it either. Milly never did any harm to anyone and she tolerated Sugden's hassling more than most would. If it had been me he was following around like a lost puppy, he'd have ended up regretting it, I can tell you that much."

Taylor looked out of the window onto the garden. The bees were flying back and forth to their hives.

"Can I ask you something?" Alice said.

"Of course." She hoped it wasn't about the honey again.

"Don't you get lonely? A young girl like you, all on your own."

"Not at all. I like my own company. Anyway, you're a fine one to talk. You live on your own."

"That's different. I'm old. It's natural for an old woman to be on her own. At least that's one thing nature got right — it's always the men who die first. You were married once, weren't you?"

"How do you know that?" Taylor was shocked.

"You used to wear a wedding ring — until quite recently, if I'm not mistaken. You can still see where it used to be."

Taylor looked at her ring finger. Alice was right. There was a slight white stripe where the wedding ring had been.

"You should be a detective," she said.

"You tend to become more observant as you get older. You're a bit more worldly-wise. What happened? With your husband, I mean."

"He died." The words startled her. She had hardly spoken about her husband since her arrival in Cornwall.

"I'm sorry," Alice said. "I didn't mean to pry."

"It was a car crash last November. He was killed instantly." It was curiously easy to talk to the old beekeeper.

"You poor thing. And that's why you came here? To get away from everything?"

"Yes."

"There's more to it than that, isn't there?"

"It's complicated."

"Isn't it always, where men are concerned? Did you know that Milly carried on wearing her wedding ring long after her husband passed away? It's probably something you youngsters wouldn't understand. Marriage was sacred in those days."

"He wasn't alone in the car." Taylor was starting to get angry. "There was a woman with him. Danny worked for a property developer in the city. The woman was a client of his. And if you believe that they just happened to be checking out a place that late at night, you'll believe anything."

Alice stood up and put her hand on Taylor's shoulder for a minute without saying anything.

"I'm over it," Taylor said, "I've moved on. I just had to get as far away from Edinburgh as possible. I like it here."

"Men," Alice mused, "they're all the same deep down. Weak, that's what they are. That's just the way it is. My Stanley promised me the earth and never failed to let me down."

"I'd better get going," Taylor said abruptly. "I don't even know why I told you all of this — I've never really spoken to anybody about it before."

"And what you've told me will stay within these four walls. It doesn't do you any good to keep it bottled up. The first time Stanley buggered off, I was in tatters. Milly had to try and put me back together again. As the years went by I soon developed a thick skin. It's what we women do. Don't give up, though. There are still a few good ones out there. Take old Eddie Sedgwick next door for example. He may be an old gossip, but he has a good heart. No, don't give up."

"When was the last time you saw your husband?" Taylor asked.

"Ten years ago, thereabouts."

"He was seen in Trotterdown last week," Taylor told her.

"Who said that?" Alice sounded rather sharp.

"A man in the Old Boar. Albarn. That was his name."

"Dennis Albarn?" Alice shook her head. "Good-for-nothing criminal. He was Stanley's best man. He's done time, you know."

"So I heard."

"It figures. Stanley would rather come and see his low-life friend than me. Probably for the best, anyway."

"I really ought to be going." Taylor stood up. "If you think of anything else that might be useful about Peter Sugden, give me a ring. You still have my number, don't you?"

"Of course. It's on the fridge with all the other important numbers."

"And thank you for listening to my babbling," Taylor added. "Like I said, I haven't really talked about it before."

"Look at us," Alice said, "what a pair we make. Two women sifting through the wreckage left by our awful husbands."

CHAPTER TWENTY-SIX

When Taylor got back to the station, DI Killian was nowhere to be seen. She went to the office she shared with DS Duncan, sat behind her desk and turned on her computer. While she waited for it to boot up, she thought about what she had told Alice Green.

She wondered why she'd opened up to the old woman.

She clicked on her emails and sighed when she saw the address on the first one. It was from the law firm that had represented her husband's estate. The whole experience had been relatively painless — Danny's will had been quite straightforward — and it was supposed to be all over.

What do they want now? I paid all the fees in full. She paused for a moment and opened up the email, which said only: 'Please see attached'.

Taylor opened the attachment and read it twice in disbelief. It was a letter from the company Danny had worked for. The deal that Danny had been working on before he died had finally been completed. Taylor, as sole heir to Daniel Taylor's estate, was due the commission

Danny had made on the deal. After the legal costs, she stood to get almost £14,000.

"Fourteen thousand," she said out loud. Just for the moment, she wasn't even sure if she wanted the money. She'd deal with it later. It was too much to think about at the moment.

She scanned her other emails. Apart from the forensic report from Milly Lancaster's car, there was nothing of interest. She printed the report and placed it in a plastic file. DS Duncan entered the room and sat down at his desk. He was sweating heavily.

"How can they expect us to work in this sauna?" He wiped his head with a handkerchief. "We need air con in here."

"It's not that bad," Taylor said. "We used to freeze to death in Edinburgh, summer and winter."

"How did the interview with Sugden go?"

"He says he didn't do it."

"Of course he does. They all say that. I'd have got him to spill the beans. I don't know why Killian insisted on having you in there."

"Where is the DI? Still at the hospital?"

"His wife's taken a turn for the worse. I hate to say it but it could be for the best."

"Why would you say that?"

"She's in for an infection, but her main problem's Alzheimer's. One of those types you get really young. She's in the advanced stages, I'm afraid."

"I didn't know."

"He doesn't shout about it, but he was even thinking of taking early retirement at one stage so he could look after her. She wasn't having any of it. She managed to persuade him to hire a full-time carer instead. It's a horrible disease."

"The poor man. I'm so sorry. D'you think one of us should be at the hospital with him?"

"He wouldn't thank us. Best thing we can do for Jack is to crack on with this investigation."

"I don't know what to make of it. I can't find any reason why Peter Sugden would want to kill Milly Lancaster."

"Bugger the motive, we've got evidence. That's enough for me."

"Hmm." She changed the subject. "Is there any more news on that body the fisherman picked up this morning?"

"Nothing. They might find out something from dental records but that'll probably take some time. I wouldn't even bother, to be honest. It's just a poor bastard who happened to run into a hungry shark."

"It wasn't a shark."

"And you're suddenly an expert on shark attacks too, are you? Haven't you got work to do? In case you've forgotten, I'm your superior officer, especially with Killian otherwise engaged. We've got two days to get Sugden to crack before we have to let him go. Let's get on with it."

Taylor was about to say something but she realised it was pointless arguing with the bull-headed detective sergeant.

"What's our next move then, sir?" she said.

"I'm going to let Sugden stew overnight and have a crack at him in the morning. Let's see how he copes with a night without nicotine. You can sit in if you want. You might learn something."

"I can't wait."

Taylor tried to concentrate on the forensic report, but she was worried about Killian. *The poor man*, she thought, *why hadn't he mentioned his wife's illness before?* She felt strangely lost without the DI around. Killian had taken her under his wing from the start. She had grown to like and respect him. He had integrity. It wasn't a quality she'd come across often, and it was very refreshing after the years of backstabbing in Edinburgh.

She skimmed through the report and then forced herself to read it again more carefully. The first section concentrated on the condition of the car. Obviously, after plummeting 25 metres over a cliff, it was a total wreck. It had landed nose first and the engine had been destroyed. The water had washed over it for some hours but Milly Lancaster's blood had still been found on the broken pieces of the windscreen and on the upholstery on the seats.

They didn't even know whether Milly was alive when the car went over the edge. Unless the body washed up, they would probably never know.

She tried to put the pieces together of what might have happened that night.

If Peter Sugden was responsible he would have had to drive with Milly up to Merryhead. How had he got back? It was a five-mile trip and Sugden didn't have a car. There was no way he could have made it back to Polgarrow unless he had help and that seemed unlikely.

Taylor read the report again. All four locks on the car had been tampered with. Even a little old lady like Milly Lancaster would have put up a fight once she realised what was happening. It would take time to jam all four locks and it would have been done one lock at a time.

Milly was already dead when she went over the edge, Taylor decided. It was the only logical explanation. Or perhaps not. Maybe Milly wasn't even in the car when it went over the cliff. Perhaps someone had made it look as if she was inside to send them off in the wrong direction.

Taylor made a mental note to bring this up when they interviewed Peter Sugden the following morning. She wanted to see his reaction. Her head was spinning from all the contradictory theories that were bouncing around in her brain. She took out her phone and tried calling Killian. It went straight to voicemail. "Jack," she used his first name for once, "if there's anything you need, just give me a call."

She looked at the time. It was almost eight. She picked up the forensic report and headed home.

CHAPTER TWENTY-SEVEN

Harriet Taylor was exhausted but she did not feel like going home to her empty house. Alice Green's words had stuck in her mind: "Don't give up."

Maybe I should try again, maybe men aren't all as bad as Danny. Or Stanley Green.

She found it curious that Alice's husband had come back and not made an effort to get in touch with his wife of forty years. *Even if he was a bastard, nobody was that much of a bastard.*

Instead of taking the coast road home, she drove inland to Polgarrow. Alice had pretended not to care that Stanley had been in the area without even popping in to say hello, but Taylor could tell that wasn't true. She was obviously very hurt.

Taylor tried the Old Boar first. She knew that Stanley's friend Dennis always drank in the pub in the evening and, if anybody knew where Stanley was, it would be Dennis. She parked outside. The late evening air was thick and muggy. Taylor had been in the south-west long enough now to know that a thunderstorm was coming.

She looked round the bar. Some young people were dancing to a live band. A couple of old men were nursing half pints of ale in the corner of the room, but there was nobody she recognised. "Excuse me," she shouted to the young barman over the music, "I'm looking for Dennis Albarn. Has he been in tonight?"

"Not yet. Sometimes he comes in a bit later. Want a drink?"

Taylor thought hard for a second.

What am I actually doing here? This is none of my business.

She decided to give Dennis Albarn an hour. If he did not show up in that time, she would leave. "I'll have a tonic and lime," she said. She took her drink to the only free table.

The band was good. The singer had an unusual raspy, bluesy voice and the drummer seemed to be lost in a world of his own, banging away on the drums like a maniac. Every now and then he would bash the cymbals so hard Taylor was scared they would break. It made her realise she should get out more, and listen to more music.

* * *

A huge clap of thunder suddenly rattled the glasses behind the bar, making Taylor jump. She checked the time. It was almost nine. She finished her drink and stood up.

"I wouldn't venture out in that, love," a man sitting by the bar warned Taylor as she walked past, "that's going to be a nasty one. I know, I've seen them like that before. I reckon the power's going to be out in a minute. You mark my words."

As he said that, the music was almost drowned out by the sound of rain hammering on the roof. The man gave Taylor a knowing smile and took a satisfied sip of his beer.

I need to get home. I'm dog-tired and a bit of rain's never bothered me. Heaven knows we have plenty of it in Scotland. She exited the Old Boar into the downpour. She was drenched in seconds, but the water wasn't cold. It was quite invigorating. Lightening flashed all around, lighting up the puddles on the road. She stood with her eyes closed, enjoying the feel of the blast on her skin and the sense of being out in the wild. Then she ran to her car and got in.

The rain was still coming down with a vengeance. She couldn't face driving through it — she was too tired and she knew she couldn't concentrate properly on the slippery roads — so she decided to wait until the storm had died down a bit. The windows fogged up inside the car.

She took off her soaked shirt and sat in just her bra. *Nobody can see me through the steamed-up windows.* She lay back on the seat and closed her eyes. She had started to drift off to sleep when the loudest clap of thunder she had ever heard made her jump so violently that she almost hit her head on the windscreen.

There was another loud bang. It shook the ground underneath Taylor's car. She knew straight away this one wasn't thunder.

CHAPTER TWENTY-EIGHT

Taylor grabbed her clammy shirt, wrestled it back on and was out of the car in seconds. The rain had relented while she was dozing. She spotted the source of the almighty blast immediately. A house up the road from the pub was on fire.

She prayed no one was inside. Killing two birds with one stone, she phoned the Trotterdown switchboard — to organise a fire engine and to get as many available officers to the scene right away. PC Eric White answered.

"Eric," she said, "I need a fire engine in Polgarrow immediately. There's been an explosion just up the road from the Old Boar pub."

"What are you doing in Polgarrow?" PC White asked.

"Just organise that fire engine," Taylor told him, "and I need as many available officers here as soon as possible. We need to keep the people away from that house. It's an inferno already." She rang off.

The rain had almost stopped. Taylor wished it would pour down again to help extinguish the blaze. She knew she should stay well back — there might be a risk of another explosion — but she approached the burning building. She was desperate to know if anyone was hurt.

The fire engine had to travel from Trotterdown. It would take it at least ten minutes to get to Polgarrow and it was clear that the only thing it could do at this stage was damage control.

The next-door cottage was at risk too. Taylor took a deep breath and pushed her way through the heat to try the front door. It opened — nobody round here locked their doors, she thought. She could just make out the shape of a man on the floor in the hallway.

"You have to get out," she shouted. There was nobody near enough to help — she'd have to try and drag him out. He was an old man, shaking, and clearly in shock. "Come on." She grabbed his arm and helped him up. "I need to get you out of here now."

She held his arm but he shrugged her off. He took a framed photograph off the wall in the hallway and followed Taylor out onto the road.

They staggered out into the choking heat and smoke. A crowd had formed outside. Everyone from the pub seemed to be there, along with others, presumably neighbours. "Everybody," Taylor shouted, "please get back. There might be another explosion. The fire brigade are on their way."

Right on cue, the sound of sirens could be heard in the distance. She reckoned they were still about four minutes away.

"Please," she shouted again, "move away from the house. If you have to watch, do it from outside the pub."

The crowd shuffled away. Taylor took the old man by the arm and walked him to the Old Boar too. He was clutching the photograph as though his life depended on it.

Two police cars arrived outside the pub just ahead of the fire engine and she went out to meet PC Thomas White and a woman she vaguely recognised.

"What happened?" Thomas asked.

"I don't know. There was just this huge explosion and the house must have gone up."

"Good lord." Thomas looked at what was left of the house.

"It's all very nice having a quaint wooden house in the country," the woman said, "but look what happens when it catches fire."

"This is Jo." Thomas was blushing. "Jo Freer. She works for Littlemore in forensics. We were sort of together when the call came through."

"What do you think happened?" Taylor asked her.

"Probably gas. I've seen it plenty of times before. Old biddy forgets to turn off the gas stove. The slightest spark would've been enough. It was probably the lightning. Old people shouldn't be allowed to own gas cookers."

"You're all heart," Taylor said.

The fire engine finally appeared. There was not much they could do now for it, but at least they could save the old man's house next door.

Thirty minutes later, it was all over. The flames were out and all that was left of the wooden house was a crumpled shell. It was obvious that everything inside had been consumed. The old man still held the framed photo in his arms.

"Are you all right?" Taylor asked him.

"I've seen worse," he said. "I'm Fred. Fred Gunnell."

"Do you have somewhere to stay tonight? I'm afraid your house will need to be checked over before you can go back."

"I can stay with Bill. He won't mind. We've been in and out of each other's houses since we were boys."

"Good. Then you'll be all right. Is there anything else you need?"

"I've got everything I need right here." Fred showed her the black-and-white photograph of a young woman. "That's my Ellie," he said proudly. "It was taken just after we were married. April. Nineteen fifty-five."

"She's beautiful," Taylor said. The young woman's smile lit up her face in the old photo.

"Thank you for coming to get me out. I really thought I'd had it," Fred said. He had a tear in the corner of his eye. "Well," he said, "I'd better be going." He turned to leave.

"Fred," Taylor said, "I'm sure your house will be fine tomorrow. It looks well built."

"Like I said, I've seen worse."

"Who's the owner of the house that burned down?" Taylor asked at last.

"That's young Dennis' house. Dennis Albarn."

CHAPTER TWENTY-NINE

Alice Green was nearly ready for bed when she heard the explosion. After the thunderstorm, she had gone outside to the garden to check on the bees. The hives were well-protected and the bees were not normally fazed by the storms, but she still wanted to make sure. She was replacing the final frame in the hive when the blast rattled the windows of the house.

Alice ran inside to see if anything had been damaged. The jackdaw was climbing up and down the bars of his cage. He was obviously very unsettled.

"It's all right, boy," Alice said. "It was probably nothing."

Her hands were shaking. She opened a bottle of port and took a long swig straight from the bottle. She had not done that in a very long time.

Sirens sounded in the distance. The explosion must have caused a fire somewhere.

She took out a glass and filled it to the brim. The sirens were getting louder. She went into the living room and opened the curtains. A crowd of people had gathered outside the Old Boar, further up the road. She spotted DC

Taylor. Her hair was drenched. She was talking to the old man who lived next door to Dennis Albarn.

Alice drained her glass and poured herself another. There was far too much commotion outside for her to even think of going to sleep. She turned on the television. The local news was on. There was no mention of the explosion.

Of course not. It's only just happened.

The leading story focused on a possible shark attack a few miles off the coast. A fisherman had pulled up the body of a man in his nets. The report was rather vague. A so-called shark expert was trying to convince the woman interviewing him that shark attacks were extremely rare and there was little chance of another attack. The reporter did not seem convinced. The weather forecaster warned of more severe storms over the next few days. They were advising people to be vigilant.

"Vigilant?" Alice said out loud. "There's nothing you can do where nature's concerned."

The port was going down well. There was only a drop left in the bottle so Alice emptied it into her glass. She was starting to feel quite drunk. She could still hear the drone of voices in the street outside. The smell of smoke drifted in through the open living-room window. Alice got up and closed it, catching a glimpse of the fire engine. It was parked directly outside Dennis Albarn's house. She smiled, finished her drink and went to the bathroom to get ready for bed.

* * *

Harriet Taylor opened the door to her house, went inside and collapsed on the sofa in the living room. Her wet hair and clothes reeked of smoke. She opened her pillbox and downed two sleeping pills. They were the last ones — she'd have to get some more pretty quickly.

She made her way upstairs and climbed under the shower. The high-pressure jets stung her scalp but she needed to get rid of the reek of smoke. She still could not take in everything that had happened that evening. She had gone to Polgarrow to speak to Dennis Albarn and now his house was burned to the ground. It didn't make sense, and yet it was surely connected in some way.

Taylor turned off the shower and dried herself. The smoky smell still lingered but her eyes were feeling heavy. She brushed her teeth and made it to the bedroom just in time. Her hair was still wet but she didn't care. She collapsed on the bed and fell asleep straight away.

CHAPTER THIRTY

The two men from the fire department entered the burned-out house at first light. The sun was rising over the ocean in the distance. There were no clouds in the sky. It was as if the storm had never happened.

All that was left of Dennis Albarn's house were the timber columns that supported the wooden roof and ceilings. Bits of charred furniture lay smouldering in the middle of what had been the living room. There was shattered glass everywhere. A metal box that only slightly resembled a cooker stood black in the corner next to one of the columns.

"There's your culprit," Geoff Harding, the station manager of the Trotterdown fire department, said to his colleague Peter Sole. "See how the stove is blacker than the surrounding floor?"

He went over to get a better look. Broken glass crunched under his feet as he walked. He picked up a small piece of jagged metal.

"I'd say this is what's left of the gas bottle," he said. "There'll be a full forensic, of course, but my guess is this. Stove left on. A spark ignites it, it travels through the pipe to the bottle — and boom, the whole place goes up. I just pray there was nobody inside when the place exploded."

"Sir," Peter Sole looked at his boss, "can you smell that?" He sounded worried. Every firefighter knew what that sweetish smell could be. "And see — that?" He pointed to something on the floor next to a smouldering armchair.

It looked like a burned pile of blankets. Sole moved closer, lifted up the edge of the cloth and retched.

The man's hair had been incinerated and his scalp was black and crispy like a piece of burnt bacon. The eye sockets were empty and the flesh around the mouth was gone, revealing a set of large black teeth. Harding swallowed hard and looked away.

"Get some fresh air," he said to Sole. "It looks like it's going to be a long day."

* * *

Taylor's mobile phone buzzed on the bedside table. She opened her eyes and winced. She had forgotten to draw the curtains before she'd fallen into bed. She could still smell smoke on the duvet and pillow. She picked up the phone.

"Taylor," said Killian's voice "where are you?"

"I'm still in bed. It's seven in the morning."

"Two guys from the fire department found a body in the house that burned down. It's not a pretty sight. I'll meet you there."

* * *

Forty-five minutes later, she parked outside Dennis Albarn's house in Polgarrow. She stared at the smouldering ruins. Killian was talking to a uniformed firefighter.

"Morning," she said. "Do we know what happened yet?"

"Looks like the gas stove blew up," the firefighter replied.

"This is Geoff Harding," Killian told her. "He's the station chief in Trotterdown. Geoff, meet DC Harriet Taylor."

"Please to meet you, Miss Taylor," Harding said. "We think the gas stove was left on and something ignited it. It would explain why everything went up so quickly."

"I heard the explosion. It was deafening. I was sitting in my car just down the road."

Killian looked surprised. "What were you doing in Polgarrow last night?"

"I went to the Old Boar. I wanted to see if I could find out more about Peter Sugden." She'd explain the full story to Killian another time.

"You work too hard."

"Do we know who was inside the house?"

"There's not much left of them," said Harding. "I suppose it'll rest on dental records. The teeth look intact."

"The house belongs to Dennis Albarn," Killian reminded her. "We actually spoke to him recently."

"I remember. How soon before we find out if it's him or not?"

"Later this morning. It turns out Albarn had some work done on his teeth when he was in prison. They're sending over his dental records as we speak."

"How's your wife doing?" Taylor asked.

"Not good, I'm afraid. They're going to keep her in for a few days to run some tests."

"If there's anything I can do, just let me know."

"Thanks. Anyway, we've got a lot to get through. If we don't get anything out of Sugden I'm afraid we're going to have to let him go."

"What about the evidence?"

"All circumstantial. His lawyer knows we have nothing concrete."

"Duncan reckons he can prise the truth out of him."

"I'm not letting him near Sugden, in the mood he's in," Killian said. "Let's get back and get it over with."

CHAPTER THIRTY-ONE

PC Eric White pounced on Killian as soon as he and Taylor walked through the door.

"Sir, we've got a positive ID on the body they found in the house. It was Dennis Albarn. No doubt about it. The dental records don't lie."

"The poor man," Taylor said. "Awful way to die."

"It looks like he accidentally left the gas on," Eric said, "and something set it off."

"How's the prisoner this morning?" Killian asked.

"Irritable. Like a bear with a sore head. He keeps moaning about not being able to smoke in the holding cells."

"Good. I want you to arrange for his solicitor to get here as soon as possible. Taylor and I are going to have another crack at him."

"I'll do it right away." White walked off.

Taylor's phone rang. She didn't recognise the number on the screen. "Sorry to trouble you," said Alice Green, "but you asked me to ring if I thought of anything else regarding Peter Sugden."

"It's no problem. What is it?"

"It didn't strike me as odd at the time, but in light of everything that's happened, I thought you might want to know."

"What is it?"

"A while ago — two or three weeks, thereabouts — I saw Sugden acting strangely around Milly's car. I didn't pay it much attention at the time."

"What do you mean by acting strangely?"

"He was lingering by it. It looked as if he was checking the doors and windows out, but he moved away quickly when he noticed me watching him. It might not mean anything but I thought you'd want to know."

"Thank you, Alice. We'll be talking to him again this morning. I'll be sure to ask him about it."

"There's something else I thought you might want to know," Alice added. "Stanley phoned last night. He asked me if I wanted to meet him."

"That's great news."

"I told him to bugger off," Alice said and rang off.

* * *

Peter Sugden was led to the interview room an hour later. His solicitor was otherwise engaged but Sugden had agreed to do the interview without him.

"I trust you slept well," Killian said.

"I hardly slept at all. I need a cigarette." Sugden looked awful. His eyes were puffy and red, with huge bags, and his face was ash-grey.

"You can have a smoke when we're finished in here," Killian promised. "I'll have one of the PCs escort you outside."

"This is outrageous, the way I've been treated. It's barbaric. I'm not a criminal."

"That's to be decided." Killian turned on the recording device. "Interview with Peter Sugden commenced ten fifteen. Present, DI Jack Killian and DC

Harriet Taylor. Mr Sugden, have you thought of anything else you'd like to tell us?"

"I didn't lay a hand on Milly," Sugden insisted. "I wouldn't hurt a fly, let alone someone as nice as Milly."

"We've already established that you were with Mrs Lancaster the night she disappeared," Killian told him. "You lied about going to the pub that night and the tool that was used to jam the locks on her car was found at your house."

"We've also had some new information come to light," Taylor added. "A while ago, you were seen hanging around Milly Lancaster's car. It looked as if you were examining the doors."

"What? Who told you that?"

"That's not important," said Killian. "If I were to hazard a guess, I would say you were trying to figure out how you could jam the locks. Did you plan all of this in advance?"

"Plan what? I don't know what you're talking about."

"Let me tell you what I think, and you can stop me if I'm on the wrong track. I think Milly made you angry when she rejected your advances and you wanted to teach her a lesson. You confronted her and things got out of hand. You drove up to Merryhead and pushed Milly and her car over the cliff."

"How did you get back that night?" Taylor asked.

"Back from where? I didn't go anywhere near Merryhead that night. I have no idea what you're talking about. I really need a cigarette."

"Not yet," Killian said. "How did you get back to Polgarrow from Merryhead after you'd dumped the car? It's a five-mile hike."

"I didn't do it. I haven't walked five miles in years." He certainly didn't look as if he could walk very far at all.

"If someone drove you back, we'll find out," Killian went on. "Why don't you tell us what happened? We have enough evidence, but I want to know why you did it. You'll feel better for it."

Taylor knew he was clutching at straws.

"I'll feel better when I've had a cigarette," Sugden said. "I'm not confessing to something I haven't done."

"Interview with Peter Sugden over." Killian switched off the machine. "You're free to go."

Sugden looked at Killian in disbelief. "I can go home?"

"Yes, but don't get any ideas about going anywhere for a while. We'll be keeping an eye on you. I'll get someone to drop you off at your home."

Sugden jammed an unlit cigarette between his lips and left the interview room.

"You don't think he did it, do you?" Taylor asked Killian.

"No. He's a repulsive specimen of a human being but I reckon he was telling the truth back there."

"What about the evidence? The screwdriver?"

"I think someone was trying to frame him," Killian said, "but I have no idea who."

"What now?"

"Back to square one. We go through what we have once more and see if anything jumps out at us."

"Three people have died in less than a week. Milly Lancaster, Dennis Albarn and the mystery man in the fishing net. We have no idea what really happened to any of them. If they're not linked, then it's even weirder. And it's driving me crazy."

"I have to get back to the hospital. Sorry. Megan will be expecting me."

"I'm sorry," Taylor told him. "I didn't know till recently that she was ill."

"It's been more than ten years now. Some days are better than others. It makes me question everything we're doing, you know. I've always believed everyone deserves a chance, but my Megan has never hurt anybody in her life and yet she's made to suffer. And there are cold-blooded murderers out there living the life of Riley."

Killian's sudden outburst took Taylor by surprise. She had never heard her boss talk like that before.

"I'm just tired." He gave her an unconvincing smile. "I'll be back in a couple of hours."

"Anything you want me to do in the meantime?"

"Kill two birds with one stone. Head down to the mortuary and see what Jon Finch can tell you about Dennis Albarn and that poor bastard who ended up in the fishing net."

CHAPTER THIRTY-TWO

It was Taylor's first time at the Trotterdown mortuary. In fact it was the first time she'd had to identify a body since Danny's. She still remembered the feeling of utter nothingness as she gazed at his face. She'd felt precisely zero, and then when she did start feeling something she'd been more angry than sad. Angry that Danny had left her alone to deal with the damage he had caused while he was alive.

Dr Jon Finch turned out to be very thin and tall. He had black hair and the most piercing blue eyes Taylor had ever seen.

"DC Harriet Taylor?" he said. "Take a seat. I have some very interesting news for you."

He smiled and his blue eyes looked even brighter. She could not help staring at them for slightly longer than was appropriate under the circumstances.

"I get them from my father," Finch said. "The eyes. They're a curse some times."

She blushed. The faint smell of aftershave lingered in the air. Taylor recognised it — Danny had worn it.

"Let's start with the man whose other half seems to have deserted him, shall we," Finch said. "Please excuse my sense of humour. I'm afraid a rather black sense of humour goes with the job."

You ought to spend some time with a certain paramedic I know, Taylor thought.

"This is certainly an interesting one," the doctor went on. He tapped a few keys on the keyboard on the desk. "Identity unknown, I'm afraid — chopped in half. It wasn't a shark attack like they're saying on the news. Sharks leave a lot of uneven jagged lacerations. This poor bugger's been sliced in half a lot more cleanly."

"I know. I saw the body. Do you have any idea how it happened?"

"A sharp piece of metal, if I were to hazard a guess. Don't quote me, though. But I do know roughly when it happened and I do know he'd been dead for quite some time *before* someone cut him up."

"How long?"

"I'd say around a week. Maybe a bit less."

"That doesn't make any sense. If he'd been in the water that long, how did he get chopped in half?"

"Ah, there's the rub." Finch clapped his hands together. "Firstly, he was only in the water a matter of hours and, secondly, he was dead before he hit the water. There was no water in his lungs and he's almost undamaged by the water. Believe me, if he'd been in the sea for that amount of time, he'd be looking very different."

"Are you saying somebody killed him, waited almost a week, chopped him up and threw him in the sea?"

"Well, it looks like it. But that's just my guess."

"OK." Taylor was finding it hard to take all of this in. "He was killed, chopped up and thrown in the sea. Do you know what killed him?"

"His brains were bashed in. Literally. He suffered a large number of heavy blows to the back of the head."

"Murder?"

"Looks like it. Somebody bashed him over the head, kept him around for almost a week and then chopped him in two. His ring finger was severed too, whatever that signifies."

"His ring finger?"

"Yes it doesn't look like it was cut off accidentally."

"What about Dennis Albarn? Surely that was an accident?"

"Mr Albarn is one of the worst burns cases I've ever come across. He had burns to over ninety percent of his body. It would have been an agonising death *if* he'd been alive before he was incinerated. But he wasn't. Just as our half-man had no water in his lungs, there were no traces of smoke in Albarn's. Fire and water. It's like something out of an opera, isn't it?"

Fire and water, Taylor thought. *What the hell is going on here?*

"If you don't mind, I have an appointment in half an hour. I'll have the reports sent over when I've finished them."

"Thank you," Taylor said. "Thank you for making things even more complicated than they already were."

"Always a pleasure." Finch offered his hand. "I'm not usually this forward," he added, "but if you should need any more information, I'd be happy to discuss it over a drink or two."

He took out a card and handed it to Taylor.

"My mobile number's on the back," he said, "should you decide to take that risk. I'm quite harmless."

"I'll give it some serious consideration," she replied.

CHAPTER THIRTY-THREE

"Murder?" Killian sank his head in his hands. "Are you saying Dennis Albarn and the man found in the fishing nets were both murdered? Are you sure?"

"Positive. Dr Finch is very thorough," Taylor said.

"What else did he give you?"

"The man the fisherman found had been dead for almost a week when he was thrown into the sea, and Albarn had no smoke in his lungs. He was dead before the explosion."

"What the hell is going on around here? First it's Milly Lancaster and now these two. We're going to be working around the clock from now on. Who else knows about this?"

"Just Dr Finch."

"Let's keep it that way for the time being. Once the press get hold of it, and they will, all hell is going to break loose. I need time to think things through before the hoards start phoning in, demanding to know what's going on."

"Do you think the three murders are connected?"

"I have no idea. What can possibly link them together?"

"Fire and water. And possibly air. Milly Lancaster's car flew through the air before she hit the rocks below Merryhead."

"What on earth are you talking about?"

"Just thinking out loud," Taylor said. "Earth, fire, water and air. The four elements, in all kinds of different belief systems."

"Are you suggesting there's some maniac out there killing people and disposing of the bodies in ways corresponding to these elements? In Cornwall?"

"I don't know. I don't know what to think. And frankly, Cornwall's probably more likely than Scotland."

"We may have our share of alternative types but they're mostly tree-huggers, not murderers. What else do we know about these three?"

"They were roughly the same age. And Milly Lancaster and Dennis Albarn knew each other."

"Everybody knows everybody else around here. It's a small community."

"Do we know anything more about the man found in the fishing nets?" Taylor felt it was her turn to start asking questions.

"No positive ID as yet. It's still a mystery."

"What about dental records, like Albarn?"

"Dental records only work when we've got something to compare those records to. We had a pretty good idea it was Albarn already. The only thing I can think of is to get a team together and start trawling through missing persons. See if anybody matching the man's age and appearance has been reported missing in the last few weeks."

"That'll take forever. We once spent two weeks on it in my last team, and we still drew a blank."

"Well, we'll have to start the process. Do you have any better suggestions?"

"Actually, I do. I saw the face. It's bloated and discoloured, but you can vaguely make out the features. I reckon a good police artist can give us an idea what the poor man looked like before he died. Then we get that image out as widely as we can."

"That's a very good idea — but we can't say we're looking for the ID of a man who was murdered, cut in half and dumped in the sea. We'd have panic on our hands."

"Shark attack, of course. Everybody still thinks it was a shark. We'll let them keep thinking that for the time being. We're looking for the ID of the victim of a tragic shark attack."

"And I know just the artist." Killian took out his phone. "Kathy Bradfield's talents are legendary."

CHAPTER THIRTY-FOUR

Eddie Sedgwick was a man of habit. He put it down to his days in the air force. He enjoyed routine. At seven on the dot, he opened his eyes, looked at Barbara on the single bed next to his and got out of bed. He went to the toilet and went to the kitchen to make some coffee. He scowled when he saw the newspaper wasn't yet on the mat by the front door.

"Bloody paperboys," Eddie said, "they keeping getting worse and worse."

He opened the door to the back garden and breathed in the cool morning air. The click of the kettle told him it had boiled. On the way back, he picked up the red pen attached to the calendar with a piece of string and crossed out the previous day's date.

"Another one bites the dust."

Eddie had been crossing off days for as long as he could remember. Barbara had said he was like a man waiting to die, counting the time he had left, but Eddie insisted it was the opposite. He was celebrating the days he had lived.

He made coffee and took it through to the conservatory. A pleasant breeze blew in through the open door. Alice Green's hollyhocks had always smelled sweeter than his. Eddie still did not know her secret and Alice would never tell him.

Eddie was lost without his morning newspaper. The first coffee of the day with an unread newspaper to take his time over was one of his greatest pleasures. He thought about phoning the newsagent to complain that the paper was being delivered later and later. Soon his wife would wake up and his solitude would be ruined. Barbara always had to talk while he was reading the newspaper.

The familiar sound of the *Trotterdown Echo* landing on the mat spurred Eddie into action. He made another cup of coffee and took both it and the paper to the conservatory.

The front page was mostly taken up by a massive photo of Dennis Albarn's house after the explosion. There was not much left of it. The words 'deadly inferno' were written in bold black letters above the photo.

Poor man, Eddie thought. He had never had much time for Dennis Albarn when he was alive but Eddie still thought it was a horrible way to die. He read the article and was slightly disappointed by the lack of details. Eddie already knew most of it anyway, thanks to the local gossipmongers who'd been working nonstop since the blaze. He gave up and turned the page.

He spat coffee all over his pyjama jacket at the sight of the picture on page three. "Barbara," he shouted to his wife, "come and look at this." He could hear her slowly getting out of bed. "Quick. Look." She shuffled in and he thrust the paper at her. "Who does that remind you of?"

"That's Stanley. Stanley Green. What's he done?"

"He's dead. He was the one they found in the fishing nets. The one who was attacked by the shark."

"Oh my." Barbara sat down. "I wonder if Alice knows about it yet."

"If she's read the paper, she knows," Eddie said. "That's Stanley Green all right, no doubt about it."

CHAPTER THIRTY-FIVE

By eight that morning, the switchboard at the Trotterdown police station had already received over one hundred calls. Half of them had mentioned Stanley Green's name. Ten percent would have been good enough. Taylor's idea had worked. Kathy Bradfield had outdone herself with the drawing. Quite a few of the people who had phoned in had commented that the likeness to Stanley Green was uncanny.

"Poor Alice." Taylor sat in the canteen staring at the picture in the newspaper.

"I remember Stanley Green," Killian said. "Bit of a wide boy, if my memory serves me right."

"I thought you said his fingerprints weren't on our system?"

"That's because he never got caught. No, he and Dennis Albarn were up to all kinds of things in their day."

"And now they're both dead." Taylor could not help staring at Stanley Green's face. His features were handsome in an old-fashioned, rugged kind of way. He bore a slight resemblance to her Danny. She could see why Alice had fallen for him in the first place. "I ought to go and see Alice," she said. "She must be in a right state."

"She'll know by now. Like I said yesterday, this is a small community. I'll send one of the Whites round to talk to her."

"I'd rather go myself."

"What's with you and the old beekeeper?"

"I don't know. She's nice. Easy to talk to. She makes a lot of sense. I think it best if I go and see her. She trusts me. Besides, both Eric and Thomas White can be a bit insensitive at times."

"Well, make it snappy. Our workload's going to be bad enough as it is. Three elderly people murdered in Polgarrow in the space of a week. The press are going to cotton on to it, soon enough. It's only a matter of time before they start asking questions."

"I'll be back as soon as I can."

* * *

Taylor was halfway to Polgarrow when she suddenly remembered something Alice Green had said the day before. She'd said he had phoned on Wednesday night wanting to meet up. But Stanley had been dead for almost a week by then.

What's happening around here? She stopped and dialled Killian's number.

"Sir," she said, "there's something that's bothering me."

"Go on," Killian said.

"Alice told me yesterday that her husband phoned her on Wednesday and asked if they could meet up. It couldn't have been Stanley. He was already dead."

"Ask her about it. Ask her if it could have been somebody pretending to be Stanley."

"There's something else. We were trying to work out the connection between the three dead people."

"You're not talking about this earth wind and fire stuff again, are you?"

"Dennis Albarn was Stanley Green's best man."

"OK," Killian said.

"Milly Lancaster was Alice's maid of honour. There were only four of them at the wedding and now Alice is the only one left."

"How do you know all of this?"

"I listen."

"Bring her in." Killian sounded serious.

"What for? Surely you don't think she's got something to do with all of this?"

"Of course not. I want you to bring her in for her own protection. Three of the wedding party are dead. Alice Green received a phone call from someone pretending to be her husband, asking if they could meet up. I think it was a trap."

"This isn't good." Taylor carefully moved back onto the road. "Why would someone want to kill three people who were at a wedding forty years ago?"

"Let's see what your beekeeper friend has to say, shall we?" Killian said.

CHAPTER THIRTY-SIX

Taylor handed Alice Green a mug of hot tea from the station canteen. "How are you feeling?"

"Numb." Alice gripped the mug with both hands. "Stanley was a piece of work but he didn't deserve this. Are you sure it was him?"

"Almost positive."

"Would it be possible for me to see him?'

"I don't think that would be a good idea. He's been dead for almost a week. I'd rather you didn't see him like that."

"What on earth happened? They're saying it was a shark attack. What was Stanley doing in the sea in the first place?"

"We don't know that yet."

"I know this is difficult," Killian joined in, "but can you think of anyone who may have wanted to hurt your husband?"

"Plenty," Alice said, without pausing to think. "Stanley trod on a lot of toes over the years."

"Enough to make someone want to kill him?"

"I don't know. It still hasn't sunk in. First Milly and now Stanley."

"And Dennis Albarn," Killian reminded her. "All three of them were at your wedding forty years ago."

"I hadn't thought about it like that." Alice looked pensive.

"The phone call you received on Wednesday night," Killian said, "you said it was Stanley. Are you sure?"

"It sounded a bit like him. I haven't heard from him in a long time, though. And the line was bad and I have to admit I'd had a few glasses of port. I was ready for bed, I think."

"What exactly did he say?"

"He said he wanted to talk. Suggested we meet up."

"Where did he want to meet?" Taylor said.

"In Trotterdown. He said that there were too many prying eyes in Polgarrow."

"But you said no?"

"Yes, I told him to bugger off. After all these years. I thought he had a nerve."

"It's good you said no," Killian said. "I'm afraid the man who phoned you wasn't your husband. It looks like it was some kind of trap to get you away. Stanley was already dead by then."

"Did he phone you on your mobile?" Taylor asked.

Alice nodded.

"Then the number will still be on the phone."

"I'm afraid I deleted it. I was so angry I wanted to remove all traces of him. How dare he come back after all this time and think he could just start where he left off? I'm sorry, I suppose I shouldn't have done that."

"It's all right," Taylor told her. "I probably would've done the same thing."

"Who do you think it was?"

"We don't know," said Killian, "and I don't want you to worry but I don't think you should be by yourself for the next few days. Not until we get to the bottom of all of this, I mean."

"Do you think somebody might want to hurt me?"

"We don't know," Killian said, "but I'd rather be safe than sorry."

"You can stay with me," Taylor offered. Killian sent her a puzzled look. "Just for a few days. I've got plenty of space, so you'd have your own room."

"I don't want to be a burden."

"You won't be."

"Ok," Killian said, "that's settled, then — but I must emphasise that nobody must know about this." He looked at Alice. "If anybody asks, you're spending a few days with a friend."

"Which is the truth, isn't it, dear?"

CHAPTER THIRTY-SEVEN

Alice closed the door and went straight through to the kitchen. DC Taylor had dropped her off to fetch what she needed. The jackdaw pecked at its cage door, meaning he was hungry. Alice emptied a full tin of dog food into the cage. The jackdaw glared at her.

"I have to go away for a few days," Alice told him sternly, "for appearances' sake. It's up to you what you do with the food. You can gobble it all up in one go or you can ration it. I'll have Eddie come in and feed you tomorrow. Eddie's all right." The jackdaw started to gobble up his food. ". . . for a man," Alice added.

She packed a few items into a small suitcase, remembering to take some honey with her as a present. She'd run out of port. She hoped that Harriet Taylor had a drop of something at her house. She's a police woman, she thought, she's bound to have something to drink. The police were all alcoholics.

She went into the garden to check on the bees. They seemed lethargic today. The sun was out and the mid-morning temperature was already in the twenties. She wondered if Eddie would also keep an eye on them for her. She was about to go back inside when she caught a glimpse of the uneven mound of earth underneath the hollyhock bushes.

That's where it all started, she thought, *almost a week ago.*

But how did it come to this? Status quo, Alice thought, *there's nothing more important than the status quo, especially in the autumn of one's life. Normality and routine above everything else. Whatever it takes.*

She smiled at the thought and went next door to the Sedgwicks' house.

Eddie was in the conservatory reading a biography of somebody she had never heard of — some man who had survived the war and had sold up everything and sailed around the world.

He looked up and took off his glasses. "Morning, Alice. They reckon it's going to hit thirty degrees today. How are you feeling? I'm so sorry about Stanley. I read about it in the newspaper."

"Don't be sorry," Alice said, "I'm not. Stanley left me years ago. I won't even miss him. That's what I want to talk to you about. I'm going away for a few days. I have an old friend in Bristol I've been promising to visit and now seems like as good a time as any, what with everything that's been going on. Would you be able to feed the jackdaw for me? You'll be doing me a huge favour."

"Of course. It'll do you good to get away from here for a few days. I'm thinking of getting away for longer than that. The bloke in the book I'm reading was fifty-nine when he sold up and set sail. It's not too late to do anything."

"You're planning to get on a boat and sail around the world? What about Barbara?"

"We can all dream. I don't want to lie on my deathbed regretting what I haven't done in my life."

"Me neither." Alice handed him the spare keys to her house. "The jackdaw gets a quarter of a tin of dog food twice a day. It's on the shelf next to his cage. I fed him this morning so he should be all right until tomorrow."

"Take all the time you need. I know Stanley wasn't around much but he was still your husband. And a shark, of all things. I'll say one thing for Stanley - he didn't do things by halves. Have a nice trip."

"Thanks, Eddie. I'd better be off. It's a long drive to Bristol."

She didn't mention the bees.

CHAPTER THIRTY-EIGHT

Harriet Taylor sat alone in her office. She had just come back from getting Alice settled in at her house. Alice had put on a brave face, but Taylor could tell she was suffering inside. Something was gnawing away at her. It had been almost a week since the hiker had found Milly Lancaster's car at the bottom of Merryhead. Milly's body had still not been found and it was highly unlikely that it ever would be. Just another body lost to the sea.

DI Killian had called a special meeting for midday. *Maybe he's come up with something,* Taylor thought, trying to stay positive. *Maybe he's figured something out.* She knew it was wishful thinking — if Killian had something he would have told her already.

There was still half an hour before the meeting so she turned on her computer and checked her emails. The law firm representing Danny's estate wanted her to get back to them. Taylor ignored the reminder and opened up the second email. It was from Dr Finch, attaching the full autopsy report for Stanley Green. He'd added 'I'm still up for that drink if you're interested.' She smiled. *Maybe I should go for a drink with Dr Finch. Maybe I should take a chance for once. What harm can it do?*

She opened the report and read it on the computer screen. Stanley Green's body had been in a mild state of decomposition when he was discovered in the fishing net. There was no water in his lungs. The sea water had barely affected his tissues and organs, which suggested he had only been in the sea a short while. The cause of death was a series of heavy blows to the back of the head. The skull was fractured in three places and the parietal lobe of the brain had suffered severe trauma. The body had been sliced in two. The lacerations were uneven, suggesting he was cut in half in stages. One of the eyes was missing and the ring finger had been removed. Barring the blows to the head, all of the other injuries had occurred after his death.

It was hardly bedtime reading. Taylor winced when she read the report again. Dr Finch's conclusion was no surprise to her. In his professional opinion, Stanley Green had been hit on the head, hidden away for around a week, chopped in half and dumped in the sea. None of it made any sense.

Why hold on to the body for so long? Why not get rid of it straight away? She was baffled. She printed the report and put it in her bag. The special meeting was about to get underway.

The atmosphere in the main conference room when Taylor walked in told her the next few hours were going to be far from pleasant. The stern faces and low mumbling hinted that a change was on the cards. A change nobody was going to welcome. Taylor sat in the seat between DS Duncan and PC Eric White. Duncan looked very pale.

"What's this all about?" Taylor whispered to Duncan.

"I don't know, but I don't like the look of it. A meeting the whole station is invited to attend can only mean crap from the top."

"Where's Killian?" she asked.

"In a meeting with the super."

"I reckon we're in for a bollocking," Eric White chipped in. "It's been a week and we're still running around like headless chickens. Three murders on our patch and nothing's been done about it."

"What? We've been working round the clock since Milly Lancaster's car was found," she said.

"And what have we got to show for it?" Duncan pointed out. "Sweet Fanny Adams."

Killian came in with Superintendent Brian Lemon, a short man in his late fifties. Taylor realised she had only spoken to him twice since arriving in Trotterdown and one of those times had been at her second interview for the DC position. A third man entered the room behind them. Dressed in an expensive-looking suit and looking stunningly sure of himself, he made an immediate impression.

"Who's that?" Taylor asked Duncan.

"No idea, but I don't like the look of him either."

"Good afternoon, everybody," Killian said into the microphone at the front of the room, "sorry to drag you away from your work. This shouldn't take long. Over to Brian."

Killian handed the floor over to the superintendent. Lemon had to lower the microphone before speaking.

"Right," he said, "good afternoon. I'll get straight to the point. As you're all aware, there's been a number of unfortunate incidents over the past week or so. Three suspicious deaths of elderly people. Three in the space of a week. I've been liaising closely with DI Killian and it appears that the investigative team have hit a brick wall of sorts."

Taylor flinched when she looked at Killian. His head was bowed. He looked like a naughty schoolboy who had been caught bunking school.

"I do not doubt your abilities as police officers," Lemon continued. "Every one of you is an asset to this team."

"Here we go," DS Duncan whispered, "we're being substituted before half time." Eric White sniggered.

"However," Lemon paused for a second, "we need to get to the bottom of this and I believe what we need here in Trotterdown, right now, are a few tactical changes. We're simply not equipped to deal with matters on this scale. People out there are already speculating about a serial killer. I've been instructed from high up to hand over the whole investigation to a team more experienced in matters like this."

The whole room radiated anger.

"I'm sure you're all aware," Lemon carried on, unperturbed, "that we can't hide away these days. We cannot afford to step out of line. The police force in general needs the support of the people we are sworn to protect."

Taylor wondered if this guy actually believed the guff that was coming out of his mouth.

"I'll hand you over to DCI Warren James from Exeter. DCI James will fill you in on the restructuring that is about to be put into place. Warren."

"Thank you." DCI James raised the microphone stand and flicked an imaginary fleck of dust from his suit. He looked too young to be a detective chief inspector but he sounded extremely confident.

"Before I begin," he said, "I can see what this looks like to you and I expect you to be resentful about that. I would be, if the shoe were on the other foot."

Nice opening, Taylor thought, you can't argue with a statement like that.

"Nevertheless, we need to face the facts. Three dead bodies and not a single lead. Let's put aside any thoughts of territorial pissing and try to work together."

Superintendent Lemon's eyed grew wide. He was obviously not pleased with James' language. Despite herself, Taylor was impressed.

"I'm not here to kick you off your own turf," James continued. "I'm here to offer you a new spin on things. New ideas and fresh minds. I won't bore you with my own track record, but let's just say, that's why I've been called in. So this is how it's going to work. A new team will be put together. The structuring will be based on how things have worked for us in the past. Most of the team will be brought in from Exeter for the duration, but we'll also need everything you can offer us too. Everybody will report to me directly. As this is not up for debate, I won't ask if there are any questions. I will be conducting the interviews for the team personally and you'll all have a chance to impress. You will be talked to during the course of the day. Thank you." DCI James turned the microphone off.

CHAPTER THIRTY-NINE

Taylor sat with Killian and DS Duncan in the canteen. Killian was halfway through his third cup of coffee in an hour. Everybody was on tenterhooks, awaiting their fate. PC Eric White had been called into Killian's office fifteen minutes earlier.

"That bastard has even taken over your office, Jack," Duncan said. "Who does he think he is?"

"He's good," Killian admitted. "Maybe he can bring some new ideas to the table."

"You can't just give up. This is our patch and I'll be damned if I'm going to let some Exeter arsehole tell me what to do."

"There's nothing we can do about it. Orders from high up."

"I can't believe you're going to take this lying down. It's not like you."

"Sometimes we have to take a step back and figure out what's important. And right now I need to be with my wife. Maybe it's for the best for DCI James to step in."

"Walk all over us, more like it. Well, I'm not going to give up without a fight," Duncan said.

"How's your wife doing?" Taylor asked Killian.

"As well as can be expected. At least her temperature's normal again. She recognised me for a while yesterday. I'm going to visit her again this afternoon."

PC Eric White announced his presence by kicking open the door to the canteen so hard it banged against the wall. He looked furious.

"That bloke is a total bastard," he said. He sat down next to Taylor.

"What happened?" she asked.

"He's only a couple of years older than me, for Pete's sake. He reckons I have an attitude problem. There's nothing wrong with my attitude. I have a great attitude."

"I take it you didn't get picked for the team, then?" she said.

"He told me I don't have enough experience for something like this." Eric shook his head. "Effing nonsense."

They sat in silence for a moment.

"You're up next," Eric said to Taylor. "Good luck. You're going to need it."

Taylor knocked on the door to Killian's office and waited.

"Come in," DCI James shouted.

It was odd to see a stranger sitting behind Killian's desk. DCI James sat with his hands clasped behind his head.

"Take a seat," he said, "this won't take long. I'm a great believer in first impressions."

And in your own importance, Taylor silently replied. She was beginning to think her own first impression of the man had been wrong.

She sat opposite and waited for him to speak first. The DCI looked her up and down. His scrutiny made her uneasy.

"You look tired," he said.

"I haven't slept much since this all started."

"And you'll sleep even less if you're selected to be a part of this team. Will that be a problem?"

"I want to find out what this is all about." She couldn't think of anything else to say.

"Good." James opened up a file on the desk in front of him. "I see you've only been in this neck of the woods for a short time."

"I came here in January."

"From Edinburgh. How on earth did you end up in a Cornish police station?"

"I needed to get away from Edinburgh. My husband was killed in a car accident last year."

"Right. And what makes you think you'll be a fit for this team?"

Taylor still had no idea what to say. She was not even sure if she wanted to be part of a team full of strangers, let alone work for someone who could pass over her husband's death with "right."

"I want to get to the bottom of all of this," she said at last. "Three elderly people have been killed in the space of a week. I've been here since the beginning, and I've been part of the enquiries so far. I know we haven't found the answer yet, but I don't think we can just discount all that work that's already been done."

James typed something on his tablet. "Do you have any theories?" He looked her in the eyes.

"One. It sounds a bit far-fetched but forty years ago, a wedding took place in Plymouth. Just four people were there, and three of them have died in the past week."

"Go on." James sounded interested. "Whose wedding? Who's the survivor?"

"Alice Green. Both bride and survivor. She keeps bees in Polgarrow. It's a small village to the south of here."

"I'm aware of it."

"The man found cut in half in the fishing net was Alice's husband Stanley. Milly Lancaster was her maid of honour and Dennis Albarn was Stanley's best man."

"Interesting." James typed away. "And you think there's some kind of connection there?"

"I think it's strange, that's all. Four people attend a wedding forty years ago, then three of them are murdered in a week."

"I'm inclined to agree with you." James stood up and looked out the window. "Killian has a nice view from his office. What do you think of Jack Killian?"

"I like him. He's a good DI. He's fair and he gets stuck in. Everybody around here respects him."

"Did you speak to DI Killian about this wedding?"

"Of course. He didn't think there was anything to it."

She regretted the words as soon as they left her lips. She had a feeling she had just helped sign Killian's death warrant.

"I see," James sat down again. "This is how it's going to work. I've always advocated the benefits of a small team. You've got to have tight lines of communication for a successful murder investigation. Obviously, I'll be heading up the team and all decisions taken will be passed through me first. DI Jane Carrick will be joining us from Exeter — she's originally from London and has many years' experience. DS Paul Southern and DC Phil Brown will be recruited for the groundwork. All in all, there'll be five of us."

"Five?"

"Unless you'd rather not join us."

"No. That's why I'm here, isn't it?"

"Good." James reached over and shook her hand. "Welcome aboard. Any questions?"

"Plenty."

"And they'll be answered in due course. Now get a good night's sleep. You're going to need it. The officers from Exeter will be arriving this evening. We'll assemble back here at 6 a.m. for a preliminary briefing. See you tomorrow. At six on the dot."

CHAPTER FORTY

Killian had already left for the hospital by the time Taylor re-joined DS Duncan and Eric.

"Is it me up next, then?" Duncan asked.

"DCI James didn't ask for you," Taylor told him. "I think he's finished with the interviews. He has the team he needs."

"So we've all been kicked aside?" said Eric. "This is bullshit."

"I'm on the team," Taylor admitted. "It seems I'm the only one from Trotterdown he wants."

"You?" Duncan said. "And what makes you so special?"

"I don't know. I didn't ask to be picked."

"You've been here five minutes." Duncan's face was getting redder and redder.

"It wasn't my decision. James asked me a few questions, I answered them and he told me I was in." She was starting to feel dizzy. She realised she hadn't eaten anything all day.

"Congratulations then," Eric said. "What are the rest of us supposed to do in the meantime?"

"Go home. Enjoy the weekend. I have to be back here at six tomorrow morning."

"How many are on the team? How many of the Exeter snobs are going to be swarming around our station?"

"Only four, including DCI James. He reckons small groups tend to get better results."

"Good luck with that." Duncan said and stomped out of the canteen.

"Ignore him," said Eric, "he's just jealous. Well done. You'll do all right. You do realise you're going to piss a few people off around here, though, don't you?"

She did. She'd realised it the moment DCI James had shaken her hand. She would be seen as a traitor. She had only recently started to be accepted at Trotterdown station. Now she would be the outsider again.

* * *

She drove the long way home, taking the coast road along the edge of the cliffs. She needed some time to think things through. On her left, the Atlantic was a lighter blue than usual. Yachts had already set out on their weekend cruises and sails of all shapes and sizes were flapping in the light breeze. She couldn't get Eric White's words out of her mind. She knew exactly what was going to happen. She'd hear muttering every time she set foot in the station. It was going to be like Edinburgh all over again.

Taylor suddenly remembered she'd run out of sleeping pills. She would need a good night's sleep before the scheduled meeting the following day. She headed for Trotterdown centre and parked her car. Tourists ambled up and down the main walkway, apparently not looking for anything in particular. Youngsters walked in groups carrying bottles of wine and boxes of beer, no doubt gearing up for the weekend. To her relief the pharmacy was still open, but her heart sank when she saw a stranger wearing the pharmacist's white coat.

"Afternoon," Taylor said. "I have a prescription here. My name's Harriet Taylor. I'm on the system. I've run out of sleeping tablets."

The young woman tapped a few keys on the keyboard and looked up at Taylor through a pair of rimless glasses.

"Hmm," she said. "This prescription has expired. You'll need to speak to your doctor to arrange another one."

"I can't. My doctor's in Edinburgh."

"Then you'll have to register with a doctor around here. You have to have a consultation first. You realise that these should only be used on a short-term basis?"

"I can't sleep," Taylor said much more loudly than she meant to. A few customers turned round and stared at her.

"I can't sleep," she repeated, much more softly this time, "please, I'll register with another doctor when I have the chance. Mr Walsh knows me. He always lets me have them."

"I'll tell you what." The queue was growing. "I'll renew it for you this time, but next time you'll have to see a doctor. These tablets are nothing to play around with."

"Thank you." Taylor's heart was pounding in her ears. She watched as the woman opened up a jar of blue capsules and emptied about twenty into a small plastic packet.

"You can't stay on these forever," the pharmacist told her. "The side effects can be very dangerous."

"I know. Just a few more weeks. I'll register with a doctor as soon as I can."

* * *

Taylor drove away from the town centre. She let out a huge sigh of relief. The pills were safely tucked away in the little box in her jacket pocket. The tension she had experienced in the pharmacy had scared her. *I'm turning into an addict.*

As she approached her house, she was surprised by the white van outside — she'd completely forgotten that Alice Green was staying with her.

When she walked in, a mouth-watering smell hit her. She was even hungrier than she'd realised.

"Hello, dear," Alice said. "Good day at work? I hope you don't mind, but I thought the least I could do was cook you something nice. There wasn't much in the freezer but I found a nice piece of gammon at the bottom."

"I don't get much chance to go shopping. That smells delicious."

"I made an apple sauce to go with it. It's an old family recipe. You didn't have any apples in the house, so I did a bit of shopping. I got a nice bottle of port too if you're interested."

"I'd better not. I've got an early start in the morning."

"On a Saturday?" Alice opened up the bottle of port and poured a large glassful.

"There's a team coming in from Exeter tonight. They'll be taking over the investigation. I'm the only one who's been asked to join them."

"That's not going to make you very popular." Alice took a long sip of port and smiled sympathetically. "Life's not going to be too pleasant for you at work, my dear."

"I know," Taylor said, "but I could hardly say no. I really need a shower. Have I got time before the food's ready?"

"Of course. The gammon's still got another half an hour at least."

CHAPTER FORTY-ONE

The hospital was a thirty-minute drive from Trotterdown. Killian knew the route like the back of his hand. He left Trotterdown behind and headed inland. The housing estates and built-up areas were replaced by open fields and smallholdings as he drove further south. The tourist season was already in full swing and Killian negotiated drivers speeding up or slowing down to a dead halt on unfamiliar twisty roads.

He thought about the day Megan was finally diagnosed. Megan had only been in her thirties when she started "seeing things funny" and being unable to do up her own buttons. It had taken a dreadful year and numerous appointments before the final diagnosis of one of the early-onset forms of Alzheimer's.

Killian had hung on to hope as long as he could. It had taken years before Megan's memory and language started to go — that was the 'good' thing about this type of the disease. He'd read every bit of research he could find, and lobbied to get Megan any and all of the medications that could help her symptoms. They'd had a decent few years. Now, ten years down the line, things were different. Megan was deteriorating, her symptoms were way beyond anything that medication could control, and she couldn't be left on her own. Once she got over this infection and came home, Killian would have to face the fact that even full-time paid carers might not be enough. He'd have to choose between putting his wife in a home, decades before he'd ever expected her to reach this stage, or give up his own work to be with his wife for the last heart-breaking years.

Maybe all of this is happening for a reason, he thought, *maybe the arrival of the team from Exeter is a sign. A sign that it's time for me to hang up my gloves and concentrate on something much more important than police work.*

Killian knew he would be able to apply for early retirement. He also knew that, under the circumstances, it would be granted. But it was a grim decision to have to make. He was thinking so hard than he almost ran into the back of a huge SUV that had come to a halt in front of him.

"Idiot," he shouted. "Watch what you're doing."

The SUV shot off at speed into the distance. Killian hated the roads at this time of year. The Cornwall tourist board claimed that the tourist revenue was essential to the local economy but, for Killian, all it meant was frustration on the roads and an increase in petty crime.

Megan was fast asleep when he got to her room. He leant over her and kissed her on the cheek. Her breathing was very rapid. Killian brushed a stray hair from her eyes and sat down next to the bed.

A young nurse came in. "She's had a pretty rough twenty-four hours," she said, "but she's quite comfortable now. She's been asleep for a few hours."

"I won't wake her. I'll just sit here if that's all right."

"Of course, Mr Killian. Can I get you a cup of coffee?" She smiled.

"No thanks. I've had far too much coffee already today."

"I thought that's how you guys solved all your cases, over endless cups of coffee."

"Something like that."

"I'd better get back to my rounds." The nurse checked the monitor next to Megan's bed. "The doctor will want to speak to you later."

"I'm not going anywhere."

The nurse left. His wife looked so peaceful in her sleep. It was as if there was nothing wrong with her. Every now and again her mouth would open slightly and close again. He shut his eyes and was just about to doze off when his phone started to ring in his pocket.

It was Taylor.

"What's happening?" he asked.

"Where are you?" she said.

"At the hospital. Megan's asleep. I was just about to nod off myself."

"Sorry. How's she doing?"

"Fine." He didn't have enough energy to talk about his wife's condition.

"I need to tell you something and I didn't want you to hear it from somebody else."

"Go on."

"DCI James wants me on his team. I thought you ought to know. I'm the only one from Trotterdown he wants."

He said nothing.

"Are you still there?" Taylor asked.

"I'm here. That's great news."

"You're not angry?"

"Why would I be angry? If he hadn't wanted you on the investigation, I would've been angry. Well done. Make us all proud."

"Thanks. I hope your wife is going to be ok."

"Thanks, Harriet."

There was a pause and then Taylor added: "There's something else. I mentioned to James about Alice Green's wedding forty years ago. I told him you thought it wasn't important. It just came out. I'm sorry."

"Taylor, my mind has been elsewhere for the past few days. You were right to mention it. Three people who were at the wedding are now dead. I should have seen the connection earlier. Like I said, my focus isn't on the job at the moment. It's time I stepped back for a while."

"Sir," Taylor said.

"Yes, Taylor." Killian stifled a yawn.

"Would it be all right if I called you if I need any help?"

"Of course. But I'm not sure DCI James will appreciate it."

"He'll never know," Taylor said and rang off.

CHAPTER FORTY-TWO

Taylor hung up.

"How did he take it?" Alice asked.

"Better than I expected. I thought he'd be angry."

"What's wrong with his wife?"

"Dementia. She's only middle-aged but she's had it for years and apparently she's pretty bad now. Killian's thinking of taking early retirement to look after her."

"See, there are still a few good men out there. Now come and eat."

The gammon was surprisingly good. Taylor hadn't enjoyed her food so much for weeks. She'd been thinking of sloping off upstairs to bed early, given how early she'd need to be up the next day, but supper gave her the energy to sit cheerily with Alice, over a glass of mint tea for her and port for her guest.

"You have a lovely house," Alice said, "it's so big. It must've cost a small fortune. Especially with that view."

"I couldn't afford it on a police salary," Taylor admitted, "but the insurance company paid out enough money for me to buy it outright. I suppose Danny looked after me in that respect."

"What was he like — Danny? He can't always have been a bad lot. You wouldn't have married him in the first place if he had been."

"Danny?" Taylor shook her head. "Danny was Danny Taylor. Everybody knew Danny. He could walk into any pub in Edinburgh and there would be somebody there he knew."

"Sounds just like my Stanley. How did you meet him?"

"It was at a Christmas party." Taylor hadn't talked about any of this since the accident. "The venue had been double-booked. Can you believe it? With all the logistical expertise the Edinburgh police force had at their disposal they couldn't even organise a Christmas do."

"It's often the way."

"Anyway, it was late December and all the decent venues were booked so we decided to share the place with some hot-shot property development company. The Royal Hotel. Smack bang in the middle of Edinburgh. I'm going to make another glass of mint tea. Would you like some?"

"I'm fine with the port. Go on. The Royal Hotel?"

"It was a typical December evening in Edinburgh. Cold, damp and dreary and looked as if it would be either raining or snowing for the next two years. They had a live band on. They were awful, but most of the guests were so drunk they didn't seem to notice. I don't drink much and there's nothing worse than watching drunk people when you're stone-cold sober. I'd had enough and I was about to slip away when I spotted a man sitting with a group of people at the bar."

"Danny?"

"Danny. He was staring at me. He wasn't making any attempt to hide it either. I must admit, I thought he was rather nice but I wasn't up for being chatted up, so I left anyway."

"Then what happened?"

"He must have followed me, because he caught up to me in the car park. He said he'd noticed I wasn't enjoying myself and asked if there was something wrong. He seemed genuinely concerned. Not creepy, just nice."

"They're all like that in the beginning. It all changes when they've got what they're after."

"We chatted in the car park for a while. I remember the rain started to come down harder and he offered me his coat. I told him I had to go and he asked me for my phone number."

"Just like that? And you gave it to him?"

"Danny was different. He made me feel different. Anyway, I gave him my number and thought nothing more of it."

"But he phoned you?"

"The very next day. I'd worked overtime and I told him I wouldn't be finished until after ten but that didn't seem to bother him. We met at a bar that stayed open late and we talked all night. Danny listened. He seemed genuinely interested in what I had to say. We were married within a year."

Alice poured another glass of port and sighed.

"What happened after the wedding?"

"That's enough of my woes." Taylor said. "It's your turn. Tell me about Stanley Green."

"It's pretty much the same story. Stanley swept me off my feet at a dance. Milly was there too, but Milly was the shy one. It's a miracle she ever found herself a husband. Stanley promised me the earth, I believed him, and we were married a month later. My family told me it would be a disaster — that's why none of them came to the wedding — but I thought it was a whirlwind romance. Prince Charming, eh?"

"Do you have any children?"

"No. Stanley said they'd only bugger things up. Those were his exact words. I thought he would change his mind as he got older but he never did."

"What did Stanley do for a living? Where did he work?"

"This and that. He never really talked much about what he did and I knew better than to ask him. There was always food on the table and I never went without. He'd be gone for days at a time. Work, he used to say. The days turned into weeks, then months and in the end he would disappear for years. The last time I set eyes on Stanley Green was ten years ago."

"But you always took him back?"

"At first I did. I knew what he was up to, but I used to fool myself into thinking, 'He always comes back to me in the end, so I must be important to him.' I pretended everything was all right. It was Milly who used to have to pick up the pieces when he left. I was a mess the first few times."

Taylor glanced at the clock on the oven. It was almost midnight.

"Is that the time?" She finished the cold tea in her glass. "I have to be up in five hours. I'd better go to bed."

"Are you sure you won't have a drop of port? It'll help you to sleep."

"I'll sleep just fine." She remembered the pills, still in her jacket pocket.

"I enjoyed the chat," Alice said. "It's nice to have someone to talk to again."

"For me too."

"You know what, Detective Harriet Taylor? You and I have more in common than either of us realises."

CHAPTER FORTY-THREE

Taylor arrived at the station fifteen minutes early. She wanted to make a good impression on her first day in the new team. DCI James was already there, talking to PC Thomas White by the front desk. Thomas looked terrified. He was a good head taller than the DCI from Exeter but he stood with his head bowed.

"Good morning. Bright and early." James had spotted her. "Good. There's time for a quick cup of coffee before we get cracking. We'll meet in my office. We won't be disturbed in there."

He meant Killian's office. James walked off to the canteen and she didn't feel like joining him. She'd made up her mind to commit to the investigative work but other than that she didn't want to be chummy with the new gang.

"Morning," Thomas said to her. "I believe you're part of the A team?"

"I won't ask what the 'A' stands for. I didn't ask to be part of this. I suppose everybody's going to snub me from now on?" she said.

"Only the morons. I say good luck to you. Get this murderer banged to rights. It's still all over the papers, you know."

"I'm sure it will be for a while yet. I suppose I'd better go and introduce myself to the A team."

Killian's office door was shut. Killian had usually left it open. Taylor didn't know whether to knock, but she did anyway. Inside, the skinniest woman Taylor had ever seen was sitting behind Killian's desk. She was wearing a pair of rimless reading glasses. DI Jane Carrick, Taylor thought.

The other two people in the room could not have been more unlike each other. One was completely bald. He had a nasty scar on the top of his head. His eyes were set far too close together and his nose was a button in the middle of his chubby face. The other was dark-skinned and pensive-looking, with green eyes and a full, almost feminine mouth.

"You must be Harriet," DI Carrick said. "Good to have you on board. I'm DI Jane Carrick and this is DS Paul Southern and DC Phil Brown."

Rather to Taylor's surprise, Brown was the bald chubby man and Southern the wistful-looking one.

"The DCI will be along in a short while," Carrick told her.

"Nice to meet you all," Taylor nodded at them.

"This must be a far cry from the bright lights of Edinburgh," Southern said. He seemed quite pleasant, she had to admit.

"Much quieter, but I like it here," Taylor said.

DCI Warren James announced his presence with a cough. Carrick stood up and James took the seat behind the desk.

"Close the door, please," he said.

Taylor closed the door. She immediately felt claustrophobic. It was as if the air was being sucked out of the room. She closed her eyes and took a deep breath.

"Are you all right?" James asked her.

"I'm fine." She concentrated on the blind behind Killian's desk. It hadn't worked properly for months but Killian hadn't bothered to get it fixed.

"Please sit down," James said. "Before we begin, for the benefit of the new member of the team there are a few things to clarify." He stared at Taylor.

"Firstly, I expect everybody in this room to give their all. Nothing less than one hundred percent is acceptable. In return, you will receive certain concessions. I've headed up a number of investigations and I've found that a few ground rules make all the difference. So for one thing, from now on, we don't mention rank."

Taylor frowned. "We don't mention it?"

"Communication on a team tends to be more relaxed if we all work on a first name basis. You are Jane, Phil, Paul and Harriet. Understood?" Everybody but Harriet Taylor nodded their heads.

"Is there some part of what I've just said you don't understand?"

"No. I understood all of it. It just makes me uncomfortable addressing a superior officer by their first name."

"Get used to it. The second point I need to address is vitally important to the success of this investigation. Confidentiality. Everything we discuss regarding this case is to stay among the team and the team alone. The last thing we need is some cavalier PC running off on his own personal crusade trying to save the day based on some titbit of info he's managed to glean from one of us. The information we choose to share will be at my discretion. Let's get started, shall we? Harriet, since you're a few steps ahead of the rest of us, why don't you tell us what you have so far."

Taylor's head was spinning. The DCI from Exeter certainly enjoyed listening to the sound of his own voice.

"OK." She put the chain of events together in her head quickly. "It all started a week ago today. Milly

Lancaster's car was found wrecked on the rocks at the bottom of Merryhead. Milly's body still hasn't been found. We suspect it was washed out to sea. We found traces of blood on the windscreen. Then the torso of an elderly man was hauled up in the nets of a fishing boat. He had been cut in half. The autopsy report indicated he had only been in the water for a few hours but he had been dead for almost a week. The body was identified as Stanley Green."

Taylor paused and looked around the room. All eyes were on her. DS Paul Southern was watching her with particularly keen interest.

"Go on," James urged.

"Then there was a huge explosion in Polgarrow. Dennis Albarn's house blew up, with him inside. It looked like an accident, because the gas stove was responsible for the blast, but Dennis Albarn was dead before the house went up."

The room was silent for a moment.

"Three dead pensioners," James said eventually, "all of them from a small village outside Trotterdown. It's all very disturbing, isn't it?" Clearly, he didn't expect anyone to answer him. They knew what they were there to tackle.

"All three knew each other well," Taylor decided to take the initiative, "which isn't particularly unusual in such a small community. What is unusual is this: forty years ago, all three of them attended a wedding in Plymouth."

"Can I stop you there?" DC Brown broke in. "Surely you can't think there's some connection between a wedding that took place forty years ago and what's happened in the past week? There must have been loads of people at the wedding."

"Let her finish," James said.

"I do think there's a connection. There were only four people at the wedding. Alice and Stanley Green, Milly Lancaster and Dennis Albarn."

"And three of them were murdered in the past seven days," Carrick said. "Where's this Alice Green now?"

"She's staying at my house. After everything that's happened I thought she'd be safer there than at home. I figured she might be next."

"Good thinking," James told her. "I'd say that gives us more than enough to be going on with, wouldn't you?"

"Have you questioned this Alice Green?" asked Carrick.

"Of course. She was one of the first people we spoke to. She's as upset as everybody else about all of this. Probably more so, as she's just lost her husband and her best friend. She's putting on a brave face but she's hurting inside."

"Bring her in again," James said.

"What for? Don't you think she's been through enough?"

"We're not going to attach electrodes to her and shock a confession out of her. I just want to get some more background on this wedding. Maybe there was someone there she didn't know about. She's the only one left from the wedding party. She may know something without even realising it. She could be the next victim for all we know. It's in everybody's best interest that we talk to her."

"Sorry. You're right. It's just . . . I've become quite close to her over the past week. She's a nice old lady. She keeps bees in her back garden."

"My dad used to keep bees," Brown said.

James glared at him. "Right. Jane, you and Harriet can speak to the beekeeper. She'll probably be more comfortable talking to female officers."

"Are we going to bring her down to the station?" Taylor was still uncomfortable at the thought of dragging Alice into an interview room.

"Yes. I want every interview recorded. That's the way it's going to be. Paul, I want you to go through all the forensics and autopsy reports with a fine toothcomb. I want to know if anything jumps out at you. Similarities in the causes of death and the like. Phil, you speak to everybody who knew the deceased. Friends, family, former work colleagues. Find out what made them tick. Take that tall PC with you."

"Thomas White," Taylor said.

"That's him. He seems to have his head screwed on. I'm going to do a bit of strategizing." He looked at the team. "I think I made the right choice here. We'll meet in the Unicorn at seven sharp to go over what we find out."

CHAPTER FORTY-FOUR

"Have you worked with DCI James for long?" Taylor asked DI Jane Carrick. They were driving to her house.

"Three years, and there's never been a dull moment. He's a bit of a stickler but he's a good boss and his record speaks for itself," Carrick replied.

"I still don't feel comfortable with this first name thing. It doesn't feel right. You're a DI, not a work buddy."

"I'll make you a deal. When this is all over, if you ever find yourself in Exeter, you'll bloody well address me as ma'am, but until then, I'm Jane. Deal?"

"Deal. And this is my house here . . . Jane."

Carrick gazed at it. "It's huge. I'm moving to Trotterdown. You guys obviously make a lot more money than us lowly Exeter plods do."

"It's a very long story."

Alice's van wasn't where it had been parked that morning. "It looks like she's gone out," Taylor said, "I'll go in and see what's going on."

"I'm coming with you. After everything that's happened we can't be too careful."

Taylor felt sick as they went in. *What if something had happened to the old lady while I was meant to be looking after her? What if she's lying dead on the floor?* Then she caught sight of the note on the kitchen fridge.

"She's gone home. She said she needed to be at home for the bees and the jackdaw."

"Jackdaw?"

"A pet. She's lived in the same place for over thirty years. I suppose it must be hard to leave."

"We still need to speak to her."

* * *

They found Alice in her back garden tending to the bees. She smiled at Taylor and looked DI Carrick up and down.

"Morning, dear," she said to Taylor. "I'm sorry, I had to come home. The bees need looking after and the jackdaw gets lonely. I left you a note."

"I saw it. This is DI Jane Carrick from Exeter."

"Exeter?" Alice stared at Carrick. "You need to eat more, love. You need a bit more flesh on your bones. I can whip up a slice of bread with some honey on it, if you like. The honey's been a bit funny lately, but I think it's still all right to eat."

"I'm fine. How many bees do you have?" Carrick said.

"Just the six hives at the moment. I'm thinking of getting some more. I sell the honey at the market in Berryton. I've got a licence, you know."

"I'm sure you have, but that's not why we're here. Can we have a word with you down at the station? It shouldn't take long," Taylor said.

"Is this about Milly?"

"In a way," Taylor said. "I'll drop you back at home afterwards."

"I'd rather go in the van. I need to pick up a few things in town anyway. I've run out of port."

* * *

Thirty minutes later, Alice, Taylor and DI Carrick sat in the interview room at the station in Trotterdown.

"Am I a suspect?" Alice said when Carrick turned on the recording device.

"No, it's the DCI's orders. He wants every interview logged for future reference. He's very meticulous."

"Would you like a cup of tea?" Taylor sat down opposite Alice.

"No, thank you. What's this all about?"

"We'd like you to think back," Carrick said, "back to your wedding day. I know it's a long time ago but I need you to think."

"It was before you two were born. What do you want to know?"

"We think what's happened in the past week may have something to do with your wedding."

"What do you mean? How could it?"

"Who was at the wedding that day?" Taylor asked.

"Me, Stanley, Milly and Dennis. I've told you all of this before."

"I know. It's just for the tape."

"There were just the four of us."

"And three of them have been killed in the space of a week," Carrick said. "Are you sure there wasn't somebody else there that day?"

"Just the clerk. We were married in a small registry office in Plymouth. It was a low-key affair. We didn't want anything flashy."

"And there's nothing else you can think of that would explain what's happened recently? Anything that struck you as suspicious at the time?"

"No. Like I said, it was very low key. Stanley and Dennis Albarn got slaughtered afterwards but that was par for the course. It wasn't much of a wedding night, I can tell you that."

"Can you think of anybody who might have wanted to hurt Stanley, Dennis and Milly?" Taylor said.

"I wanted to kill Stanley and Dennis plenty of times myself, but poor Milly? She wouldn't hurt a fly. I suppose I shouldn't have said that on the tape, should I?"

"It's all right, Alice," Taylor told her. "You're not a suspect here. We're exploring a number of avenues at the moment and this wedding is the best we've come up with so far. It's all we've got to go on."

"Nothing happened. We said 'I do' and that was it."

"OK," Carrick said, "where did you go after the wedding? Did you have some kind of a reception?"

"We went to this dive in Plymouth. It was Stanley who organised it. He and Dennis got legless. We left at around ten and went home."

"In Plymouth?" Taylor said.

"That's right. We had a small flat above a baker's shop. We moved to Polgarrow a few years later."

Carrick paused the machine. "Thank you for your time."

"I'm sorry I couldn't help you more, but I still can't see how our wedding has anything to do with what happened to Stanley, Milly and Dennis."

Carrick turned the machine on.

"When was the last time you saw your husband?"

"Ten years ago. More or less."

"Ten years? That's a long time. Where did he go?"

"I don't know and I don't care. Stanley has been out of my life for years. I'm not even sure I feel much about his death."

"That's understandable," Taylor said.

"I've got used to being on my own. I like it that way. I've got my bees. They're all I need."

"Alice, you told me that Stanley phoned you on Wednesday night."

"That's right."

"But he was already dead by then. That means it was somebody pretending to be your husband. Do you have any idea who it might have been?"

"I was a bit tipsy. I'd had quite a lot of port. It sounded like Stanley, but the line was bad. It could've been Dennis Albarn for all I know. He and Stanley had similar voices."

"Dennis Albarn?" Carrick said. "Why would he phone, pretending to be your husband, and arrange to meet?"

"Maybe as a joke. Dennis never liked me, and the feeling was mutual."

"Albarn's house blew up with him in it on Wednesday at half past nine," said Taylor. "What time was the phone call?"

"It was before the explosion. I know, I heard the blast."

"So Albarn could've phoned you?" Carrick said.

"Let's take a break," Taylor suggested. "This is all getting confusing."

"I think we're finished here anyway." Carrick switched off the recording device. "Thank you, Alice. You can go now."

"Will you be OK on your own?" Taylor asked.

"I'll be all right." Alice looked at Taylor. "I've got your number if I notice anything suspicious going on. I'll make sure my doors are locked."

"I don't think you need to worry," Carrick said.

When Alice had left the room, she turned to Taylor. "I've got an idea. It's a bit of a wild stab in the dark, but it's worth looking into. What if Dennis Albarn is behind all of this? What if he killed Stanley Green?"

"Why? Why would he kill his best friend?"

"Stranger things have happened. Maybe they had a drunken argument that got out of hand. Maybe Albarn saw red and killed Stanley Green. Milly Lancaster saw the whole thing and Albarn had to get rid of her to shut her up."

"What about the explosion?"

"An accident? Maybe Albarn was overcome by guilt, he tried to gas himself but ended up dying in a much more spectacular fashion? Like I said, it's just a wild stab in the dark."

"No, the more I think of it, the more it makes sense. Albarn can't have been banking on the worst lightning storm in years to happen when he left the gas on. With a house full of flammable gas, it wouldn't have taken much to set it off. Now all we have to do is try to link Albarn to Stanley Green and Milly Lancaster."

"And if we can, we're left with one small problem. Dennis Albarn is dead. He'll have got away with it."

"Hardly. He must have had a horrible death. What now?"

"Let's wait and see what DS Southern finds out from the forensic reports. I'm particularly interested in that fire."

CHAPTER FORTY-FIVE

DS Paul Southern was sitting by himself in the canteen. It was fairly busy, but nobody had joined him. Taylor could sense the tension in the room when she and Carrick walked in. She did her best to ignore it, and sat down at Southern's table.

"Did you find anything?" Carrick asked.

"I don't know. I've pretty much figured out the timescale. The chain of events goes something like this. Stanley Green was killed first. Cause of death was a severe blow to the head that caused a fractured skull and splinters of bone into the brain, and he was cut in half afterwards. We can assume Milly Lancaster was next even though her body still hasn't been found. Dennis Albarn was the last one."

"What about the fire report?" Taylor said. "Have you been through it?"

"Of course. The gas was left on, that much is clear, and it does seem to have been set off by a direct lightning strike. Albarn wouldn't have stood a chance."

"Do you think it was an accident?"

"Yes. Just a dreadful set of coincidences. An old guy forgets to switch the gas off and a freak lightning flash hits the house. What are the chances? One in a million?"

"I don't buy it," Carrick said. "I want to have a look at the report myself. We'll need Albarn's DNA too. I want to see if we can link him in any way to the deaths of Stanley Green and Milly Lancaster."

"You can't be serious?"

"Deadly serious." She told him her theory and he thought about it for a moment.

"You know what, you could actually be onto something there."

"Dennis Albarn's phone," Taylor said. "Was it found among the wreckage?"

"Everything was destroyed. You saw the place. It must have been a hell of a blast."

"It was. I was just nearby when it happened."

"Why do you want his phone?"

"He may have phoned Alice Green on Wednesday evening, shortly before the explosion. Alice deleted the number. She thought it was her husband, but he was already dead by then."

"We don't need the phone, then. We just need to get hold of his service provider. All the calls will be logged."

Taylor could have kicked herself for not thinking of that herself. With everything that had happened, she had lost sight of standard procedure. Nevertheless, she had the feeling that they were starting to get somewhere. The new team from Exeter seemed to be the catalyst they desperately needed.

They were joined by an exhausted-looking DC Brown. "I'm knackered," he said. "We must have harassed half the population of Polgarrow today. Those old people really know how to chat."

"Did you find anything?" Carrick asked.

"Stanley Green and Dennis Albarn were well-known characters. Well, more notorious, really, but more loveable rogues than anything worse. Everyone we spoke to said the same thing. Nobody could think of any reason why somebody would actually want to kill them."

"What about Milly Lancaster?"

"That's a strange one. Nobody had much to say about Milly Lancaster at all. She kept herself to herself, by all accounts. Alice Green was her only friend."

They sat in silence for a while. Taylor turned to look at one of the other tables. Two PCs she barely knew were scowling at her. "Is there something wrong?" she shouted over at them. The pair got up and left the canteen.

"We've got two hours before the meeting with the DCI," Carrick said. "I want forensics to go over everything again but I need to run it past James first. It's been a long day for everyone, so I suggest we all go and freshen up a bit before we have to meet in the Unicorn at seven."

Taylor grabbed the opportunity to get home, even only for a short time. She found a jar of honey on the kitchen table. She was sure it hadn't been there when she and Carrick had been there earlier.

Alice still has my spare keys, she thought, making a mental note to pick them up when she had a chance. She opened the back door and went into the garden. The late afternoon sun was beating down on the distant sea. She'd never tire of this view. She would much rather have stayed here than go to the Unicorn. She knew full well that the pub wasn't a place for the faint-hearted on a Saturday night. The clientele could be rather rowdy and there always seemed to be trouble around closing time.

Taylor's phone rang.

"Hello, Alice," she said.

"How did you know it was me?" Alice replied.

"Caller ID. What's wrong?"

"Nothing. I just wanted to thank you for letting me stay at your house. And I've had a think about the phone call I received on Wednesday evening. I think you might be right and it could well have been Dennis Albarn. It's such a shame I deleted the number."

"It doesn't matter. We can find out if he phoned you anyway. All his calls will be logged with his service provider."

"Oh."

Taylor realised that for someone of Alice's age, modern technology might be hard to fathom sometimes. She certainly sounded taken aback.

She rallied pretty quickly and suggested she bring back Taylor's keys later.

"I'm afraid I have to go out."

"Oh yes? Tell me you've finally bitten the bullet and decided to go out on a date?"

"No, we've got a case meeting at the Unicorn at seven. You can drop the keys off at the station tomorrow, if you like."

"Tomorrow's Sunday. Don't tell me they've got you working on a Sunday?"

"I'm afraid criminals don't work a five-day week. I'll tell you what. I'll fetch the keys the next time I'm in Polgarrow."

"That's fine, dear. Enjoy the meeting," Alice said and rang off.

Taylor went upstairs and ran a shower. She made it as cold as she could handle, blasting freezing cold water onto her head. It revived her, and her mind started to race.

Could Dennis Albarn have killed Stanley Green and Milly Lancaster? She thought. Was it really that simple? DI Carrick's theory was becoming more and more credible, the more she thought about it.

She got out of the shower and dried herself. She was wide awake and ready for the meeting. Unicorn or no Unicorn, they were going to get results, she was certain of it. She glanced at her reflection in the mirror. Her eyes were bloodshot and there were dark rings underneath them. Her skin was deathly pale. She remembered the £14,000. She had a couple of weeks' holiday owed to her.

When this is all over, she thought, *I'm going to take a holiday somewhere. Somewhere warm and far away.*

* * *

The Unicorn was already busy at a quarter to seven. Groups of young people sat at tables laughing at the screens of mobile phones. Older patrons sat at the bar nursing pints of ale. Taylor found the team from Exeter at the table furthest from the bar. DS Southern wasn't there yet.

"Take a seat," DCI James said. "Brown's buying. What do you want to drink?"

"Tonic water, please."

"Are you pulling my leg?"

"No. I don't drink."

"You call yourself a detective?" James patted DC Brown on the shoulder.

"You heard the lady," he said to the pig-faced DC, "she'll have a tonic water. And I'll have another pint."

Brown shuffled off towards the crowded bar. DS Southern arrived and sat down next to James. He was wearing far too much aftershave and had a small plaster on his chin where he had obviously cut himself shaving.

"Right," James said when Brown had returned with the drinks, "let's get started. Jane?"

"We've come up with something. I think it's worth checking out."

"Good. That's what I like to hear. Go on."

"Dennis Albarn. What if he killed Stanley Green in a fit of rage? And Milly Lancaster happened to witness the attack so he killed her to shut her up."

"Mmm. And then you think Albarn topped himself out of remorse for what he'd done?"

"Exactly. What do you think?"

"It's a bit far-fetched but I've seen real situations that were more bizarre. What made you come up with this?"

"The gas. I think he meant to kill himself by sticking his head in the oven, but the lightning had other ideas."

"Alice Green had a phone call on Wednesday evening too," Taylor added. "The night of the explosion. She thinks it was Albarn who phoned her. First she thought it was her husband, but he was already dead by then. We'll need your go ahead to contact Albarn's service provider to check."

"Good." James finished half the beer in his glass in one go and belched. "Excuse me. Phil, what did you and White find out from knocking on doors?"

"Not much. Nothing suspicious sprang out."

"Then we'll go with Carrick's theory for the time being. I'll need forensics to go over everything again, taking into account the new info we have. What's the grub like in this place?" He looked at Taylor.

"I've never eaten here. I very rarely go out."

"Young lass like you? What a waste. I'm starving and Trotterdown is paying. What's everyone having?"

They all settled for fish and chips. James sent Brown back to the bar to place the order.

"What's the plan, boss?" Carrick asked him.

"I eat my fish and chips and then I down as many pints as my stomach can handle." He drained his glass to demonstrate. "You mean the plan for tomorrow? We shake things up a bit. I, for one, would love Albarn to be our man. Done, dusted and he's copped it to boot. We need some hard evidence to back it up. Fingerprints on Milly Lancaster's car. A weapon in Albarn's house with Stanley Green's blood all over it."

"Albarn spent time inside," Taylor said. "His fingerprints will be on file."

"Good. Tomorrow, we're going to put a firecracker so far up the forensics guys' arses, they're going to be walking bow-legged for weeks."

"Littlemore's going to love that."

Their fish and chips arrived and they all focused on the food. DC Brown finished first. He ate like he hadn't seen food in weeks. Taylor barely touched hers. Something was bothering her. There were still holes in the story, and here they were, celebrating as if they'd closed the investigation. Taylor wondered what DI Killian would make of it all.

He's probably in the hospital, she thought, *at his wife's bedside, while we're out enjoying ourselves. It wasn't right.*

"Right then," James pushed his empty plate to the middle of the table, "this is what's going to happen tomorrow. We'll drag out Albarn's phone records. See if he phoned Alice Green before he went and topped himself."

"Maybe he phoned her to confess," Southern suggested, "to clear his conscience before he died."

"But why pretend to be Alice's husband?" Taylor asked.

"We don't know," said James. "No doubt we'll find out and if we don't, too bad. Let's confirm that he actually did phone her and then we'll let forensics do their thing. I'm personally going to be on their backs the whole time. If everything goes to plan, by Monday, it'll be case closed. Polgarrow will be able to sleep easy, and I'll go back to Exeter."

He punched the air and Taylor cringed. She hoped her feelings weren't too obvious, but she couldn't help it. She had a sudden urge to get out of there as quickly as possible.

"Would it be all right if I went home? I'm exhausted. I really need to catch up on some sleep."

"And miss out on the party?" James said. "You'll stay right here. We're only just getting started."

"Harriet's right." Carrick came to her rescue. "We have a lot to get through tomorrow and we all need to be up bright and early with fresh heads."

"On you go, then," James said, "don't let me stop you. I'm going to stick around for a bit though. I like this place."

"Thank you." She didn't want to give him a chance to change his mind. "I'll see you all tomorrow."

CHAPTER FORTY-SIX

Taylor felt a lot better once she got home. She had just needed to get away from the Unicorn. DCI James' voice had given her a headache. The more he drank, the worse he got. She was regretting agreeing to join the team from Exeter, not least because she was faced with a no-win situation. If DI Carrick's theory turned out to be right and they managed to crack the case in less than two days, the Trotterdown police would appear incompetent. Taylor's life would be extremely unpleasant for weeks, if not months afterwards. On the other hand, if they found nothing to link Dennis Albarn to the murders and the investigation dragged on, everybody would think she'd jumped onto the wrong ship. She'd be the station laughing-stock.

The best case scenario would be if she worked it out on her own. And there was pretty well no chance of that.

Something had changed in her house. She couldn't put her finger on it — just a sense that something was different. She shrugged it off and made herself some cheese on toast. Her appetite had returned, now she'd left the pub. The jar of honey was still on the kitchen table.

She put it in the cupboard. She'd never dared tell Alice, but she hated honey.

Poor Alice, she's been through so much heartache in her life. Imagine being married to a man who disappeared for years on end. Danny's accident had spared her that at least.

She took her plate through to the living room. The cushions on the sofa were arranged differently. She put them back the way they had been and sat down.

Let's go back to the beginning, she thought.

DI Carrick's theory was convenient but Taylor's gut told her they were focusing all their efforts on the easiest solution for the investigation. She found a piece of paper and a pen and started to write:

> Stanley Green, found on Wednesday 17 June in the nets of a fishing boat. Dead for almost a week. Date of death therefore around 10 or 11 June. Dennis Albarn claims he saw Green in Trotterdown on Wednesday 10 June and they agreed to meet that Friday.

Albarn might have been the last person to see Stanley Green alive. That tied in with Carrick's theory. Albarn could have met Green, killed him and lied about meeting him in Trotterdown that Friday.

> Why chop him in half and dump him in the sea almost a week after killing him?

> Milly Lancaster, last seen Friday 12 June. She didn't show up for market on the Saturday and her car was found at the bottom of Merryhead on Sunday 14 June.

Maybe Albarn forced her to drive up there and pushed the car off the cliff. Albarn was reasonably fit so the walk back to Polgarrow would have been no problem for him.

She looked back over her notes. On paper, everything supported Carrick's theory but surely it couldn't be that simple?

Dennis Albarn, she wrote and underlined the name. She wondered what had been going on is his head.

> Killed in an explosion Wednesday 17 June. The gas was left on and the lightning caused a spark that blew up the whole house. Stanley Green's body was found on the same day.

What were the chances of that happening? One in a million? So . . . Dennis Albarn didn't expect the body to ever be found, panicked and saw only one way out?

Taylor gave in. DI Carrick must be right and they had found their murderer. She finished her cheese on toast and started getting ready for bed. She flipped her pillbox open and frowned. She was sure there had been more tablets in there. Maybe the new pharmacist had given her fewer tablets than usual. She swallowed two of the blue capsules, climbed into bed and waited for the dreamless nothingness to take over.

CHAPTER FORTY-SEVEN

The longest day of the year brought with it such an influx of tourists to the area around Trotterdown that the roads were already gridlocked when Taylor set off at six-thirty. She'd never experienced anything like it before. Summer in Edinburgh had been busy, but nothing like this. It was starting to get horribly hot and sticky inside her car, and when she wound down the windows, the air outside was not much cooler. The car in front moved forwards slightly, only to grind to a halt after a few seconds. She turned off the engine, afraid it would overheat.

This is all I need. I'm going to be late. She took out her phone and dialled the station switchboard. PC Eric White answered immediately.

"Eric, it's DC Taylor. I'm stuck in the worst traffic jam I've ever seen."

"Welcome to Cornwall. It's the solstice. Everybody wants to be in the West Country for the solstice. You don't want to be at Stonehenge today. I heard they've already had four accidents around there."

"I'm supposed to be at a meeting at seven and I'm going to be late. Could you do me a favour and let DCI James know?"

"OK," White said cheerfully and rang off. The traffic in front of her slowly started to move.

She turned the engine on and eased forward. Her speedometer told her she was travelling at five miles per hour. The clock on the dashboard read seven already. She turned on the radio and tuned it to the local station. A droning voice was telling people to stay off the roads because a heatwave was on the cards and a record number of visitors were expected. The longest day of the year really was going to be a long one for DC Harriet Taylor.

* * *

She got to the station just before eight. She was already exhausted and the day had barely started. She made her way to Killian's office, knocked on the door and went inside. DCI James' expression indicated he was not impressed.

"Sorry I'm late. The traffic from my house was a nightmare," she said.

"It's the twenty-first. The longest day. You should have made allowances. Everybody else managed to get here on time."

"I didn't realise the roads would be that bad."

"A phone call would've done." James sounded as if he were telling off a small child.

"I did phone. I phoned the switchboard. I asked PC Eric White to let you know."

"Then it must have slipped his mind. Anyway, now you've deigned to join us, we might as well get cracking."

Taylor sat down next to DS Southern. Eric had wanted to get her in trouble. She'd have a word or two with him before the day was through.

"You haven't missed much," James said, "fortunately for you. We're all still inclined to agree with Carrick's theory. It's the only way forward, as we stand."

"I agree. I went through it again last night. The sequence of events points to Dennis Albarn. The timescale fits."

"Then let's see if we can prove it." James sat back with his hands clasped behind his head. "A dead man can't be tried, but we still need some concrete evidence if we're going to make this wash with the general public."

"And the press," DC Phil Brown added. His piggy eyes were even more sunk into the sockets and his chubby face was blotchy.

"Phil," James said to him, "since you're looking the shittiest out of all of us, you can take the easiest job. Get hold of Albarn's service provider and get a log of all the calls made and received in the past week. You really ought to know your limits with the drink. Jane, you come with me. Let's see if this Littlemore bloke is as good as he's supposed to be."

"What about us?" Southern asked.

"I want you and Harriet to search through what's left of Albarn's house. I believe the fire department's said it's safe to enter. You might want to think about a change of clothes."

Great, Taylor thought, *I'm being punished for being late.* Eric White is going to pay dearly for this.

* * *

The traffic on the roads had eased off slightly as Taylor and DS Southern made their way towards Polgarrow. It was still oppressively hot, though, and Taylor knew it was only going to get worse. She was sweating in the old tracksuit she'd found in the lost property room. Southern had decided to risk it and was still wearing his own clothes.

"He likes you," he said, "DCI James. He definitely likes you."

"It doesn't feel like it. How come he's making us dredge through what's left of the house? Surely he could have got a couple of rookie uniform guys to do it?"

"They wouldn't know what they were looking for and they wouldn't know what to do with it, even if they did find something."

"What exactly are we looking for? I thought everything in the house was destroyed."

"Most of it was. I read the initial forensics report but they may have overlooked something. It happens all the time. Besides, Albarn wasn't a suspect at the time."

"This feels odd. Investigating the murders of two people in a house where our main suspect died. It doesn't seem right, somehow."

"If he did do it, we need to know, and if he didn't, we still need to know."

"Wise words, but I have a feeling it's not going to be that easy."

"How long have you been in CID?" Southern asked.

"Since January. I came here from Edinburgh."

"Then you must have had your reasons." He stopped the car outside of what was left of Dennis Albarn's house.

"It still stinks," Taylor said as they approached the burned-out shell.

"I expect they'll have to knock it down and start again. Wooden houses are all very well and nice to look at, but I wouldn't fancy the maintenance. And look what happens in a fire."

"Where do we start?"

"The front door is always a good place." Southern got out a pair of rubber gloves and Taylor did the same. "At least where the front door used to be."

They explored the house, broken glass crunching underfoot. Everything was black and charred and most of it was unidentifiable. Taylor was glad she had put on the old tracksuit. It was filthy in seconds. She wished she had changed her shoes as well.

"The things we do in the line of duty, eh?" Southern smiled at her. His perfect teeth looked even whiter against the layer of soot that had formed on his face.

* * *

"There's not much left," Taylor said after half an hour of searching. "This has been a waste of time."

"Let's check the garden and then we can call it a day." He wiped a bit of grit from his eye.

Dennis Albarn's back garden consisted of a long stretch of unkempt lawn with a table and two small chairs on a concrete slab at the bottom. A tiny tin shed stood next to the table and chairs. It appeared to have survived the explosion intact.

"Albarn wasn't much of a gardener, that's pretty clear," Southern said. The shed was locked with a rusty iron padlock, which looked as if nobody had touched it in quite a while. "And how on earth are we going to get into that?"

"Give me a moment." Taylor went back into the house and came out with a piece of metal. She picked up a brick from a pile next to the garden wall. "It's a spring from one of the burnt chairs," she explained.

"What are you going to do?"

"Don't ask." She banged the furniture spring with the brick until it straightened out a bit, put the sharp end in the keyhole of the lock and hit the other end as hard as she could with the brick. The lock sprang open with a click.

"Scottish skeleton key." She held up the metal.

"I've seen everything now." Southern shook his head.

"I grew up in an interesting town. A lot of my friends were boys." She took the lock off and pushed the shed door open.

The smell hit the two detectives at the same time and both of them recoiled. A malty stench with a certain sweetness to it.

"Home brew." Southern pointed to the crates of empty beer bottles on the floor of the shed. Two large barrels stood next to them.

"My dad used to make this stuff. I'll never forget that smell. My mother hated it."

"There's not much else in here," Taylor said. She stepped inside. Apart from paraphernalia associated with home brewing — pots of yeast, bottles of sugar and various tubes and pipes — there was not much else inside the shed. There were no tools to indicate that Dennis Albarn had any interest in gardening.

"This place is just a mini brewery," Southern said.

A sudden gust of wind blew in from a slit in the window opposite them and slammed the door shut. On the back of the shed door, supported by two rusty nails was a large green shovel. And this one obviously had been well-used. So well-used, in fact that the paint on the blade had been scraped off in places and the metal was dented. Its edge, though, looked sharp and nasty.

CHAPTER FORTY-EIGHT

"A shovel in a shed full of brewing equipment!" DCI James was beaming from ear to ear. "No other tools, just the shovel with a very sharp edge. The same implement our forensics friend Littlemore claims was used to chop Stanley Green in half. If there's any traces of Stanley Green on that shovel we can put this one to bed and get back to civilisation. How do you put up with those bloody tourists, by the way?" He looked at Taylor.

"I haven't been here long enough to have an opinion either way," she replied.

"How long before we know?" Southern asked.

"An hour or so. I've made it clear that the shovel is their main priority at the moment."

"I still can't believe it," said Taylor. "Carrick's hunch was spot on."

"Jane is very astute. And don't sell yourself short — you're not unlike her, if I may say so. There may be a promotion on the way in the near future. I, for one, would be happy to have you on my team."

Over my dead body, Taylor thought.

"This waiting is driving me crazy," Paul Southern said.

"Patience, Paul," James said. "We'll get there in the end. We always do."

"What did Phil find out from the phone log?" Southern asked.

"Waste of time. Albarn didn't phone Alice Green that evening."

"So who phoned Alice, then?" Taylor said.

"It was probably a prank call. Like our beekeeper said, she was half-cut at the time and the line was bad. I wouldn't be surprised if the whole thing was in her imagination. You know how old people can be at times."

"So Albarn didn't use his phone on Wednesday night?" said Southern.

"Who cares?" James' smug smile was getting wider. "It's all irrelevant now. When the shovel you found matches the one used to chop Stanley Green in half, we'll be home free."

"Are you sure there were no calls on his phone on Wednesday?" Taylor was finding it hard to believe that Alice Green had got it wrong. She was getting on a bit, but there was nothing wrong with her mind.

"I've got the call log here," James produced a piece of paper.

Taylor looked at the log. There was one call at seven thirty-five.

"Somebody called him. Do we know who it was?"

"We traced it to a phone box in Trotterdown, so it could have been anybody. I really don't think it matters. My gut feeling is telling me that Dennis Albarn is our man."

"Mine too," Southern agreed.

"Make that three of us," DI Carrick entered the office, "a woman's intuition is rarely wrong."

Taylor smiled even though she was still not convinced. These detectives from Exeter were already basking in the glory of their success and looking forward to buggering off back home as soon as they could.

Leaving me to pick up the pieces. DCI James' team had succeeded in making a fool out of the entire Trotterdown police department in the space of a few days. It would be Taylor who would be left to face the music. Well, she hadn't finished yet.

"Let's say the shovel is the one used to chop up Stanley Green. Who's to say it wasn't planted in Albarn's shed?"

"Come on," James said. "Of course it might have been, but who'd want to frame him? There's no evidence. Whereas the timeline fits perfectly. Albarn was in all the right places at the right times. The man's a known felon, for Pete's sake. Enjoy a well-deserved victory when it comes along."

"They'll get over it," Southern said. "Your colleagues, I mean. OK, there'll be some sour grapes, maybe plenty of them, but you have to rise above it. The worst that will happen is you'll have to put up with a few scowls and glares. You might get the silent treatment for a while, but you'll have a lot more respect around this place afterwards. I can promise you that."

"Paul's right," James agreed. "Bugger the lot of them. They're not worth bothering about. I reckon we celebrate tonight. My shout, and I'm not taking no for an answer."

"Let's see what forensics have to say first," Taylor said. "I'm going to shower and change my clothes. I can still feel the soot on me."

"What's her problem?" James said as she left the office. "She should be pleased."

"It's going to be tough on her for a while," Southern replied.

"Bollocks," James said.

CHAPTER FORTY-NINE

Taylor called DI Killian. With everything that had happened, she had almost forgotten about his wife's illness. Killian answered straight away.

"Sir, how're you doing?"

"Rested. The doctors sent me home last night and I had the best sleep in a long time," he said

"How's Megan?"

"Stable."

"Can we talk?"

"Of course. What's on your mind?"

"Not over the phone. Can you meet me up at Merryhead in an hour?"

"Merryhead? Why do you want to meet up there?"

"I don't know. I suppose that's where all of this started. I need you to help me with something. I can't think straight at the moment."

"Merryhead it is, then," Killian said.

Taylor dumped the soot-covered tracksuit at the front desk with DC Eric White.

"What's this?" he asked.

She had a sudden idea. "I'm running late and this is the tracksuit we found at Dennis Albarn's house. It needs to be treated carefully, bagged and labelled. I'd do it myself but, like I said, I'm late."

"What do you want me to do with it?"

"Bag and label it, and send it down to evidence. Oh, and the soot is important so make sure you don't lose any of it."

Taylor left him to it. She glanced behind and chuckled as White held the tracksuit like a newborn in his attempt to preserve the precious soot. *Maybe next time you'll pass on a message when I ask you to,* she thought.

She left the station before anybody had a chance to stop her. The roads were much quieter now. Maybe all the tourists had taken refuge from the heat. She could relax and try to work everything out. On the one hand, if Dennis Albarn had killed Stanley Green and Milly Lancaster and then committed suicide, it meant the case was closed and everybody could get on with their lives. DCI James and his team from Exeter could leave them in peace and Killian could get his office back. However — and the doubts were still nagging at Taylor's insides — if Albarn wasn't guilty, it meant that somebody had murdered three people and framed Albarn. And that meant there was a murderer — a clever one — still at large.

* * *

Killian was already parked at the top of Merryhead when Taylor arrived. He was leaning against the door of his car, staring out over the cliff top at the Atlantic.

"It makes you think, doesn't it?" she said. "Makes you realise how small and insignificant we all are."

"It makes me glad to be alive. What's on your mind?"

"DCI James thinks we've cracked the case. We found a shovel in Dennis Albarn's shed. It's probably the one that was used to cut Stanley Green in half." She told Killian everything else that had happened.

"But that's great news," Killian said. "You did it. You showed them."

"Aren't you upset that it wasn't you who solved it?"

"Who cares who solved it? It's all over."

"I'm not sure. Something doesn't feel right."

"From what you've just told me it all fits. I don't particularly like DCI James, but he doesn't make mistakes."

"I suppose you're right. Maybe I just didn't want him to be the one who figured it out."

"It's a result. That's all that matters and you were part of it. Don't forget that."

"That's another thing that's worrying me. People have been treating me differently. They're acting like I'm some kind of traitor."

Taylor's phone rang in her pocket. "Taylor," said PC Eric White, "DCI James couldn't find you anywhere. He wanted me to let you know they found Stanley Green's blood on the shovel you found in Dennis Albarn's shed. It looks like it's all over."

"Thanks, Eric."

"One more thing. Nobody seems to know anything about the tracksuit you asked me to take down to evidence. My shirt's filthy from that thing. I got a real bollocking from the super about it."

"Sorry. I must have been mistaken."

She rang off and grinned.

"It looks like you're going to get your office back," she told Killian. "Forensics have confirmed it. The shovel found in Dennis Albarn's shed was the same one that was used to slice Stanley Green in half."

"That's that, then. Everybody wins. We've found our murderer, we don't have to spend taxpayers' money on trials and incarceration, and we'll all see the back of DCI James and his motley crew."

"He wants to go out and celebrate tonight."

"Just go. Enjoy the fruits of your hard work. Southern and Carrick aren't too bad."

"I suppose you're right. I can go for a couple of hours. There's something else I need to ask you."

"You're pushing your luck now."

"I'm exhausted. I have some leave owed to me and I was thinking of taking some time off. I was wondering if you would approve a couple of weeks."

"Consider it done. And now, if there's nothing more, I have to get going."

"There is one thing. You're not really thinking about taking early retirement, are you?"

"Have a nice evening, Taylor." Killian walked back to his car.

CHAPTER FIFTY

Taylor was glad DCI James had not chosen the Unicorn to celebrate the end of the investigation. She didn't think she could handle the place two nights in a row. The car park of the Parade Hotel was almost full when she drove in. She parked next to an old VW camper van that obviously belonged to a group of keen surfers, with three surfboards tied to the roof. The tourist season was definitely in full swing.

Taylor thought about her own holiday. She really needed a break. In fact, she couldn't remember the last time she had been away. Danny was always too busy doing whatever he did to even think about a break. She realised the last time she had been out of the country was on her honeymoon. That was a brief stay in a dreary hotel in Paris. Danny had needed to get back to work after a few days. After that, Taylor had spent most of her annual leave on her own in their house in Edinburgh.

I wasted three years of my life on that bastard. It's time I lived a bit for myself.

She heard the team inside before she saw them. DCI James was particularly loud. Taylor almost turned round and left. Then she remembered what Killian had said —

she would endure a few hours with the detectives from Exeter and leave. With any luck she would not have to set eyes on Warren James ever again.

"Harriet," James shouted. He was holding a pint in one hand and what looked like a large whisky in his other. He was obviously already very drunk.

Here goes, Taylor thought. She walked up to their table. DS Southern stood up as she came closer.

"Glad you could make it." He offered her the chair next to DI Carrick, "I took the liberty of ordering you a drink. Tonic water, wasn't it?"

"Thanks." *Maybe this wouldn't be so bad, after all.*

"Now we're all here," James stood up unsteadily, "I'd like to make a toast. Everyone raise your glasses. Exeter and DC Harriet Taylor, you've done me proud."

Taylor took a sip of tonic water. She was completely unprepared for what happened next.

"And as for Trotterdown," James downed his whisky, "Fuck Trotterdown."

Half the room turned to see what was going on.

"Fuck Trotterdown," James was not finished yet, "we came, we saw, and we bloody well conquered." He finished the beer. "Fuck Trotterdown," he said again under his breath and belched.

"How much has he had to drink?" Taylor whispered to Southern.

"He started as soon as the results came in from forensics," Southern muttered. "He has a bit of a problem."

"What are you two whispering about?" James said. "Another round? I'm buying. It's all on me. Two days, I tell you, two days and we nailed it. How long do you think you lot would've taken to figure it out?"

His glazed eyed tried to focus on Taylor's face. He smiled at her. "Two years?"

She'd had enough. She couldn't help herself.

"Warren," she said, "it's all right if I call you Warren, isn't it? I'm still not convinced this investigation is over."

Everyone at the table stared at her in disbelief.

"Come again?" James said.

"Something's bothering me about it. Something's not quite right."

"Bothering you?" He stood up and teetered from side to side. "Bothering you? The only thing bothering you is that you lot are so inept that you had to beg for our help."

"And we're grateful for your help." She now wished that she'd kept her mouth shut. "I just need to check a few things before I'm happy about all of this."

"You'll do no such thing." James thrust his head forward aggressively. "This investigation is over. It's been put to bed. You do not want to make an enemy of me, Constable."

He said the last sentence with such venom that she flinched.

"Take it easy, boss. We're here to celebrate." Carrick's attempt to calm the situation fell on deaf ears.

"Who the hell do you think you are?" James glared at Taylor. "And do you know who I am? Detective Chief Inspector Warren James. Youngest DCI in the history of the Exeter police department. I have the best clear-up rate in the west of England. And you are?"

"I think you'd better leave," Southern said. "He gets like this sometimes. He'll come and apologise in the morning."

Taylor stood up and left without saying a word.

As she drove away from the Parade Hotel, Taylor shook off James' little outburst. It hadn't surprised her and it had given her an excuse to leave. It was still early and she wasn't tired. It was still light on this never-ending longest day.

She didn't feel like going home. A reckless idea suddenly struck her — she decided to take a risk for once in her life. She found the card in her purse, took out her phone and tapped in the number.

CHAPTER FIFTY-ONE

Dr Jon Finch entered the Old Boar pub in Polgarrow, stooping to get through the low door. His hair was wet. He'd obviously had a quick shower after Taylor had phoned him. She waved to him from the table closest to the bar.

"Dr Finch. Sorry to drag you out on a Sunday evening."

"Are you kidding? Drinks with a charming lady beats Antiques Roadshow hands down. And please call me Jon."

Taylor laughed. Finch was wearing the same aftershave as when she'd first met him. Danny's aftershave. Something Italian, she recalled.

Finch got them both drinks — her usual tonic water, a pint of lager for himself — and joined her at the table. "I believe congratulations are in order. You ought to be out celebrating."

"News travels fast around here. And I'm done with the celebrating thing. It didn't go down too well."

"Cheers anyway," Finch took a sip of his lager. "I wasn't expecting you to call, to be honest."

"I bet you give your card to all the ladies. And false modesty doesn't suit you, especially with those eyes."

"I told you. They're more of a curse than anything else."

"I need a favour, Jon."

"Interesting. The case is closed, so you're not here in a professional capacity. What sort of favour are we talking about here? We barely know each other."

"Very charming, I'll give you that. Dennis Albarn, the man who died in the fire, I need to have another look at the autopsy report."

Finch's bright blue eyes darkened slightly and he pursed his lips.

"You said to ask if I ever needed to discuss anything with you."

"I'm playing with you. I've perfected the 'petulant child' pout. What do you need to know about the report?"

"I don't know but there's something bugging me about this whole thing."

"I'll have it sent over first thing in the morning. Will there be anything else? I do a great John Wayne impression if you're interested."

"Maybe later. Could you send it to my home email address, though?" She took out one of her cards and wrote the address on the back.

"Is this going to get me into trouble?" Finch put the card in his back pocket. "I was told the case was closed."

"It is. I just need to make sure everything fits together first. It's for my own peace of mind more than anything else."

"Then I'd be happy to help. But do yourself a favour and keep this quiet. I've worked with James before and he's not known for his tolerance when it comes to people going off on their own. He's arrogant, but that kind of conceitedness doesn't just materialise out of nothing. James' record speaks for itself."

The door to the pub opened and Alice Green walked in. Spotting Finch and Taylor, she grinned widely.

She brought a glass of port over to their table. "Hello, my dear, lovely to see you again."

She glanced at Finch and then sent Taylor an enquiring look.

"Sorry," Taylor said. "Alice, this is Dr Jon Finch. Jon, meet Alice Green, a friend of mine."

"It's a pleasure to meet you, Alice." Finch stood up and held out his hand.

"Oh my," Alice said, "look at the size of you. I bet you bang your head on things all the time. And those eyes, look at those eyes. I am sure you were a real terror when you were a child."

"Would you care to join us, Alice?" he asked.

"No, I wouldn't dream of disturbing you." She smiled at Taylor. "I still have your spare keys. I can fetch them now if you like. I only live a few doors down."

"It's all right. I'll pick them up next time I'm in the area."

"You two enjoy your evening." Alice winked and went to the other side of the bar.

"She's quite a character," Finch remarked. "How on earth did you become friends with her?"

"Alice's husband was the one who was found in the fishing nets. I've spent quite a lot of time with her over the past week or so. I've grown to like her a lot. We have quite a lot in common."

"Poor woman, it must be awful for her. She seems to be handling it quite well though."

"She hadn't seen him in ten years. She pretends not to care, but I think she's hurting inside. Even though she hides it well."

Finch's phone started to vibrate in his pocket. He took it out, looked at the screen and frowned.

"Answer it, if you like," Taylor told him.

Finch left the pub to take the call.

"Sorry," he said when he returned, "I have to go. Duty calls. Nasty case needs tackling now. I'll send the report over to you first thing in the morning. Thank you for the company. I really enjoyed it." Without further explanation, he left.

"I want to know everything." Alice was at Taylor's table as soon as the doctor had exited.

"There's nothing to tell, honestly. Dr Finch is a colleague. He's a pathologist."

"A what?"

"He examines bodies. Finds out what happened to them."

"What a horrible job. Who would want to do such a thing?" She sat down at the table. "You don't mind, do you?"

"Of course not." She wasn't sure if she should tell Alice about the outcome of the investigation.

Alice spoke first. "I want to ask you something. Tomorrow's my birthday. I'd love it if you could come and celebrate it with me. What with Milly gone and Eddie and Barbara not being much company, I'd only end up spending it on my own with the jackdaw. I'll cook us a lovely meal. Maybe a nice joint of beef. Unless you've already made plans."

"No, I rarely have plans. It sounds great."

"Six o'clock, then." Alice smiled.

"There's something I need to tell you." *She's going to find out sooner or later,* Taylor thought. *It'll be in all the papers tomorrow, so it'll be better if she hears it from me first.*

"We've found the man responsible for Stanley's and Milly's deaths," she said.

"Oh my."

"It looks like it was Dennis Albarn."

"Dennis Albarn?" Alice looked shocked. "But he died in the fire."

"It appears he killed himself."

"But why?" Alice drained her port in one go. "Why would Albarn do such a thing? Stanley was his best friend and Milly never did anything to him."

"We're unsure as to the details, but we think Stanley and Dennis got into a fight, it got out of hand and Albarn killed your husband. We can only assume that Milly witnessed the whole thing and Albarn disposed of her to keep her quiet. Then Albarn's conscience got the better of him and he killed himself."

"By blowing his house up?"

"I don't think that was meant to happen."

"So it's all over?" Alice said. "I don't have to worry about being the next victim?"

"No. But are you all right? This must be quite a shock for you."

"I always knew Albarn was a bad lot," she said. "I don't know what to think, to be honest. I'm just relieved it's all over. We can all get back to normal again. You don't realise how important it is to preserve the status quo when you get to my age." She looked stunned. "I'll see you tomorrow at six," Alice said, and hurried off.

CHAPTER FIFTY-TWO

Taylor knew it was going to be chaos at the station when she arrived but she was totally unprepared for what she encountered. A huge crowd of reporters had gathered outside. Some of them had even camped out for the night, by the look of things. Several TV crews had set up and she'd have to run the gauntlet to get to the station door. She braced herself for a barrage of questions.

"DC Taylor!" A man held a microphone so close to Taylor's mouth, she was tempted to take a bite out of it. "What was it like working on such a complex case?"

"No comment." They'd get their information soon enough from the press conference.

"I believe you were the only one from Trotterdown involved in the investigation?" asked a young woman.

"Everybody here was involved. And I'm from Edinburgh."

Where do they get their information from? she wondered, and barged past them inside the station.

The two PCs White were deep in conversation by the front desk. They stopped talking as soon as Taylor walked in.

"Get over it," she said and went on walking. "It's all over." She carried on down the corridor towards the office she shared with DS Duncan. He was staring blankly at his computer screen.

"Morning, Sarge."

"I can't figure this thing out." Duncan pressed keys helplessly. "Ugh. No idea what's going wrong."

"What are you trying to do?"

"I'm trying to send an email and every time I send it, it comes back telling me it's bounced."

"Let's have a look," Taylor bent over his shoulder. "There's your problem. You're sending to 'com,' not 'co.uk.'"

"Thanks. It always gets me, that one. Congratulations on the investigation, by the way. You did us all proud."

Taylor wasn't sure she had heard correctly. "Are you all right?"

"I've got a bit of a cold."

"No, you realise you've just paid me a compliment?"

"You did well. I give praise, where praise is due."

"Thanks, Sarge."

Taylor headed to the canteen for a cup of tea. Duncan's words had cheered her up as much as they'd surprised her — he was the last person she expected to congratulate her. Her high spirits disappeared when she walked into the canteen and saw DCI Warren James sitting by the window with Carrick, Southern and Brown. They had the whole room to themselves.

"There's our girl." James' voice echoed. He had obviously forgotten about the scene he had caused in the hotel the night before.

"Sit down," he told her. "We're going through our strategy for today. Don't worry, you're in good hands. I've done this plenty of times before."

"Strategy?" Taylor sat next to DC Brown. "I thought the case was closed."

"You'll soon learn — case closed is often just the beginning. Now comes the gauntlet that is the fourth estate."

"The press," Carrick clarified.

"I know what the fourth estate means," said Taylor.

"Nowadays," James continued, "solving the crime is just one aspect of our jobs." Clearly, one of his lengthy soliloquies was on the cards. "The crimes have been solved and now we have to make sure we're seen in a favourable light. Our PR is as important as the rest of our performance."

This idiot really does love the sound of his own voice, Taylor thought.

"We all need to be on-message." James was far from finished. "We need to be singing from the same song-sheet. We'll be running through our key points and making sure we're all coordinated. Sorry about last night, Taylor, by the way. I tend to get a bit over- enthusiastic when an investigation is wound up."

Is that the apology Southern was talking about? He might as well not have bothered.

"As I said," James went on "we have the whole day to prepare ourselves. The press office has a few ends to tie up — press materials and whatnot. So we've called the press conference for six this evening."

"I can't make it," Taylor said, "I've got plans." She was due to celebrate Alice Green's birthday with her.

"Cancel them."

"I can't. I promised."

"You will be at that press conference." James said. "You were part of the team. Your presence is required. You were the representative of Trotterdown in all of this. Your colleagues are relying on you."

Taylor was stuck. She didn't want to let Alice down but her whole career could go up in smoke if she didn't do what he said.

"I'll be there." She'd have to find a way to let Alice down gently.

* * *

The next three hours were possibly the most painful of Taylor's life. By the end, she was exhausted and still none the wiser about the right and wrong way to address the press. After the first hour of James' lecture, she almost dozed off. Only the subtle nudge under the table from DS Southern had kept her awake. When the ordeal was over, everyone was given the rest of the day off to 'get themselves ready' (Warren was clearly heading for a haircut before facing the cameras). Taylor headed straight for Killian's office.

He was staring out of the window when she knocked and entered.

"Back to normal again," she said. "It's good to see you back in here."

"It's good to be back. I suppose you're here about your leave. I haven't forgotten."

"I was thinking about two weeks starting tomorrow."

"No problem. Planning on getting away?"

"Definitely. A nice break somewhere warm and far away."

"I envy you. I can't remember when I last had a proper holiday. That's all a bit in the past for Megan and me."

"How's she doing?"

"Better. She may be allowed home in the next few days. It's not right at home without her. I'll send the leave forms through to admin. I believe James has organised the press conference for six this evening?"

"Yes. I'm dreading it. I've got a feeling he's going to parade us in front of the press like prize cattle."

"Smile and wave. It'll be over before you know it."

"If you say so. I'll see you there."

"I'm not invited. It'll be fine and then you can enjoy a well-earned break. We'll miss you around here."

Taylor left past PC Eric White in reception without saying a word. There were still hours before the press conference. She got in her car and drove straight home, where she turned on her computer. Dennis Albarn's autopsy report was the only new email. She opened it and read it carefully.

Albarn had suffered extensive burns to most of his body. His internal organs had been boiled by the intense heat. Taylor shuddered. She read the whole report and scrolled back up to the top. There has to be something here, she told herself. She read it again. Albarn's heart had stopped beating before he was engulfed in flames. She didn't understand some of the terminology. She took out her phone and dialled Dr Finch's number.

"Finch," he answered. He sounded tired.

"Jon," Taylor said, "can you talk?"

"Have been able to since I was eighteen months old. That's twice in two days you've phoned me. What can I do for you?"

"I'm reading the autopsy report now. Can you translate something for me?"

"Hold on. Let me get to my computer."

She heard rustling on the other end of the line.

"Are you still there?" she asked.

"Just clearing my desk a bit. Fire away."

"There's something here that doesn't make sense."

"Which part?"

"Inhalation analgesia negative. What does that mean?"

"When the central nervous system is shut down by some external cause, it loses the ability to function. The receptors that normally allow us to feel pain are basically turned off. It's called analgesia — pain relief. But Albarn's central nervous system didn't do this."

"Once again in English, please."

"OK, try this. Dennis Albarn's heart didn't stop beating as a result of the fire or the gas in the house."

"How did he die, then?"

"I'm afraid the body was in such a state there wasn't much left for us to go on. The only thing I can say for certain is that he wasn't killed by the explosion or by gas inhalation."

"And the team from Exeter are aware of this?"

"Of course. They had access to all the reports."

"Thank you. I owe you a drink."

"I'll hold you to that. Call me any time."

CHAPTER FIFTY-THREE

What the hell was going on? Taylor left her computer and went outside for some fresh air. In a few hours' time DCI James was going to stand in front of a hoard of journalists to bask in the glory of a successful investigation. There was no way she could tackle him before the press conference — her life wouldn't be worth living. On the other hand she wasn't sure she could sit through a press conference full of self-important pronouncements when she knew for a fact they were nothing more than speculation.

She needed something to take her mind off everything. For some reason she remembered the annoying law lecturer with his "Dr Livingstone, I presume" attempt at a joke, and she grinned. She went back to her desk, took a deep breath and emailed her bank details to the company who owed her Danny's commission. Then she booked and paid for ten days on a small boat going up the Nile.

This time on Wednesday I'll be far away from everything, I may not find the source of the Nile — and it looks as if I won't find the solution here either — but at least I'll be doing something completely new.

Buoyed up by her decisiveness, she decided to go into town, buy Alice Green a birthday present and drop it off. She could spend a few hours with her and then go on to the press conference.

* * *

It was easy enough to find a bottle of fine port — she couldn't go wrong with that — and she even found what she hoped was a suitable card to take over to Alice's house in Polgarrow.

She exchanged a few words with Eddie Sedgwick, who was pruning his roses in his front garden, and knocked on the door. Alice opened it, looking rather confused.

"Hello, dear, but you're rather early. I haven't even put the roast in the oven yet."

"I'm afraid I won't be able to make it. I've been told in no uncertain terms that I have to attend a press conference at six. I'm sorry, I couldn't get out of it."

"That's all right, love. Come in. Is that for me?"

"It is. Happy birthday. I didn't know which one you normally drank."

"Not this one." Alice examined the label. "This is the expensive one. I'll have a drop or two of that later."

"I hope I haven't put you out." Taylor followed her inside. "I only found out about the press conference a few hours ago."

"Plans change. I learned that a long time ago. Would you like some tea?"

"That would be lovely." She sat down at the table in the kitchen and Alice busied herself with making tea.

"Morning," the jackdaw shrieked. "Morning."

"He hasn't learned how to say afternoon yet. It's a shame about the press conference, but I suppose all your hard work ought to be recognised."

"It's hardly recognition. I'm dreading it. That DCI from Exeter is an arrogant egomaniac."

"Men. Too much testosterone. They never grow up, really." She poured the tea into two china cups and handed one to Taylor. "So it's all over? It's back to normal again? Apart from Milly not being around, that is. Albarn is going to rot in hell for what he did."

"It . . . yes, it is." *I'm here to celebrate her birthday*, Taylor thought. *And she seems so relieved. I can't tell her my misgivings.*

"So what about that lovely beef, then?" Alice changed the subject. "When can you make it?"

"Tomorrow? The minute this press conference is over, I've got two weeks off. I'm flying out on Wednesday for a ten-day trip up the Nile."

"How lovely. And you've earned it. You deserve a holiday. Tomorrow sounds perfect. Come at lunch, since you're not at work? And I'll make us a nice pudding too."

CHAPTER FIFTY-FOUR

Even though Taylor arrived at the station an hour before the press conference, the car park was already full and news crews were setting up outside the building. It was going to be a long night, with the biggest story to hit the local news in — well, possibly ever.

The two PCs White and DS Duncan were standing by the entrance as she went in. Eric White spotted her, tapped his namesake on the shoulder and they both started to clap. DS Duncan joined in. She could feel her face turning red.

"Stop it," she told them. "It's embarrassing."

"You're famous," Thomas White said. "You're going to be in all the papers."

"I'm dreading it. DCI James is going to make a whole song and dance about it — I'm sure of it."

"James is an arsehole, but you have to admit, he gets results," Duncan said.

"I can't wait for it to be over. I'm off up the Nile on Wednesday."

"Lucky bugger," Eric said.

"Is Killian here?"

"He was headed up to the canteen last time I saw him."

"Well, I need a cup of tea." She didn't, but she wanted to see him.

She found Killian sitting by himself in the canteen. "All set?" he asked her.

"No. Journalists make me panic."

"I'll let you in on a trick I learned a long time ago," Killian said. "When you're in front of a large group of people, don't picture them as people."

"Don't tell me. Imagine them naked?"

"That's ridiculous. No, when you see all the faces before you, imagine they all have faces like pigs."

"Pigs?"

"With their tiny eyes and hairy snouts. It works for me."

"I'll give it a go." The idea amused her. "I've got a feeling the DCI is going to do most of the talking anyway. James really loves the sound of his own voice. Anyway, I've booked a ten-day cruise up the Nile. I'm leaving on Wednesday."

"Just what the doctor ordered. Send me a postcard."

"At least tomorrow we'll be free of the Exeter crew. I can't wait for things to get back to normal again."

"Things are never normal. You have to accept that there will always be something new happening. Don't get old before your time."

She checked her watch. "Here goes. Wish me luck."

"I wish I could be there, but James made it totally clear I'm not welcome."

"You're lucky. And I'm still not so sure this is all over."

She left Killian looking slightly perplexed. It was still early when she got to the conference room but James and the other Exeter detectives were already behind the desk and the press officer was starting to look slightly frantic. She slid in at the end, beside DS Southern.

"I thought you weren't coming," James hissed. He looked extremely polished. Taylor was pretty sure he was wearing foundation.

"It's not six yet."

The room started to fill up. It looked as if there were journalists from every newspaper and news channel. The press officer switched on the microphones and nodded to the speakers.

"Good evening." Superintendent Lemon cleared his throat. "Thank you all for coming. I'll keep this brief. The man of the moment, DCI Warren James, will provide you with all the information you need in due course. I'm sure you're all aware of the protocol. Any questions you have will be answered at the end. Over to you, Warren."

"Thank you." Warren James leaned forward to his microphone.

Taylor could feel the eyes — not to speak of the cameras of scores — panning the desk. *Pigs,* she thought, *they're all pigs with beady eyes and long snouts.* She looked at a man in the front row and did her best to picture him snuffling in the trough. It helped a bit.

"Good evening, everybody," James began, "I'm sure you're all aware of the tragic events of recent days. The small peaceful village of Polgarrow is still mourning the loss of three of its elderly residents."

He paused for effect. It was obviously a rehearsed tactic. The journalists leaned forward, eager to hear what he was going to say next.

"Three elderly people have died," he continued, "all in the space of a week and all under suspicious circumstances. The Trotterdown police department pleaded for our help."

Pleaded? Taylor gritted her teeth as he took them slowly through the whole story, trying not to wince or look dubious as he explained exactly why Albarn was the murderer. Finally, he finished and smiled at the crowd. "We've cleared up this investigation, and I trust the community can sleep easy again." He looked around the room.

What's he waiting for? Taylor thought. *A round of applause?*

"I'm sure you all have questions," James went on, "but first I would like to introduce you to the team who made this all possible. If it weren't for them, I wouldn't be here in front of you today." He gestured to Taylor and the detectives from Exeter. Taylor wanted the ground to swallow her up. She couldn't remember a time when she had felt more uncomfortable.

"DI Carrick," James said, "DS Southern, DC Brown and Trotterdown's own DC Taylor. It was a pleasure working with you."

Taylor prayed the journalists were not going to give them a round of applause.

"Any questions?" James asked before they had a chance.

"DCI James," the man Taylor had pictured as a pig said. "George Harrow, *West Country Herald*. How's the relationship between Exeter and Trotterdown, now that you've had to come to their rescue?"

James paused for a moment and then picked up smoothly. "I wouldn't say 'rescue.' We enjoyed their support throughout this investigation. My team are — how can I put it — way ahead in the experience stakes when it comes to this type of crime, that's all."

"Could I ask DC Taylor if she feels the same way?" He looked at Taylor.

"Of course," James said. She tried to look calm.

"DC Taylor, what was it like to abandon your colleagues and jump to another side? How do your workmates feel about you being the only one from Trotterdown chosen to work on the investigation?"

"As far as I'm aware," Taylor said as steadily as she could, "this was not an individual crusade. We've all been working together to bring the investigation to a conclusion. As far as I'm concerned, this was a team effort. It's never been about individual glory."

"Not even for DCI James?"

"Not even for DCI James."

James was clearly trying to suppress a look of fury, and DS Southern one of distinct amusement. Taylor smiled as blandly as she could.

The questions moved on to the other details of the case. Taylor was exhausted by the end of it. At least Killian had been spared the press conference, and James' barely-disguised hints at his incompetence. Taylor hoped the journalists would leave that part out of their stories.

"That went well," James told his team before being dragged off for the cameras.

"You can keep the glory," Taylor said. "As far as I'm concerned we were just doing what they pay us to do."

"Come on, you need to be able to maximise an opportunity like this! How do you think I worked my way up?"

Narcissistic tendencies? Taylor thought to herself. "I have to go," she announced. "As of now, I'm officially on leave for two weeks. It was interesting working with you."

She walked away before they said anything.

CHAPTER FIFTY-FIVE

Harriet Taylor woke up from a dreamless sleep to the sound of rain beating down on the roof. Something was bothering her. DCI James and his team would no doubt be back in Exeter by now, wallowing in the glory of a successful investigation and spreading stories about the incompetence of the Trotterdown police department. The case was closed and it was all over.

But Dennis Albarn hadn't killed Milly Lancaster and Stanley Green.

She went down and made coffee, enjoying the luxury of a late morning in her dressing-gown. Rain lashed against the window and she found she was rather enjoying that too. Tomorrow morning she'd be on a flight, and then onto the boat that would take her up the Nile. Ten days discovering a new place was exactly what she needed. For now, she had a couple of hours to kill before the lunch with Alice Green and nobody to tell her what to do. She went upstairs to run a bath.

* * *

A couple of hours later, she knocked on Alice's door. The rain had cleared and she felt distinctly cheerful. They might not have cleared up the case to her complete satisfaction, but she was determined to put it behind her. Perhaps they'd been right after all.

Alice called her through to the back garden, where the bees were buzzing back and forth from the hollyhock bushes to the hives. They looked extremely busy.

"They're back to normal," Alice said. "They had me worried for a while when they were making that honey that wasn't quite right."

"Is there much to beekeeping? It looks quite complicated."

"There's nothing to it. The bees do most of the work for me. My bees are Italian and rather slothful but I like them that way. I'll show you."

She approached the hives and lifted off the first frame. Taylor stood back cautiously.

"They won't hurt you. They die if they sting and they know it."

Taylor moved a step closer and watched the beekeeper slide a sheet of honeycomb out of the frame.

"That's better. I'll have plenty for market at this rate." She slid the honeycomb back and then suddenly winced.

"Are you all right?" Taylor asked.

"Little bugger stung me. It happens sometimes. It's not serious. I have some bicarb solution in the drawer in the kitchen. Would you be a love and fetch it for me? There's some cotton wool in there too. It's starting to throb now."

Taylor went inside and opened the drawer in the kitchen. She rummaged around and found the bicarb solution. It was in a small, clearly labelled bottle. The cotton wool was harder to track down. She opened the drawer wider and finally found it underneath a packet of plasters. She was about to close the drawer when something caught her eye. It was a gold wedding ring and it looked like a man's one.

Taylor picked it up and took a closer look. The initials S. and A. and the numbers 14-6-75 were etched on the inside.

Stanley and Alice, Taylor thought. This is Stanley Green's wedding ring. What's her husband's wedding ring doing in the drawer?

She suddenly felt sick. Stanley Green's ring finger had been missing when they found his body.

Think fast. What's going on here?

She put the ring back in the drawer and was about to close it when she got the feeling that somebody was watching her.

"Did you find it, love?" Alice stood in the doorway.

"I've got it here." Taylor closed the door. *Had Alice seen her find the ring?* She handed Alice the bee-sting solution and the cotton wool.

"Are you all right, Harriet?" Alice asked. "You look a bit pale. I'm the one who was stung."

"I'm fine," Taylor said. "It must be the past few weeks catching up with me. The cruise will do me good."

"I'm sure it will." Alice looked at Taylor and then at the kitchen drawer. She dabbed some bicarbonate of soda on the sting and put the bottle on the kitchen counter. "The food's ready."

"It smells delicious."

It did, but Taylor felt quite sick at the prospect of eating anything. "Could I just use your bathroom first?"

"First door on the right." Alice pointed towards the corridor.

Taylor locked the door, sat on the edge of the bath and took a deep breath. She tried to think of a reasonable explanation why Alice might have the ring in her kitchen drawer. Perhaps Stanley had merely given it back to her, but then what about the missing ring finger? Perhaps it was Alice's, but it looked too big, and Alice wore a similar gold band on her ring finger. She flushed the toilet and took out her phone. She brought up Killian's number and paused, thinking hard.

What am I doing? This is ridiculous. Alice Green is an elderly beekeeper. She wouldn't hurt a fly. She put the phone back in her pocket and went back to the table.

"I hope you don't mind," Alice told her. "I thought seeing as though you're not going to be at work for two weeks, you might join me in a glass of port. I know you don't usually drink but this is a special occasion, isn't it?"

"One glass won't hurt me. Thank you. This looks delicious."

"Take a seat. I'll carve the beef."

She slid out a chair and Taylor sat down. She watched as Alice carefully sliced into the meat. The knife looked extremely sharp. She put three slices on Taylor's plate.

"Help yourself to some vegetables. I've got some gravy on the boil too."

She tore off a piece of fat and slid it into the bottom of the jackdaw's cage. The bird eyed it suspiciously, pecked at it and gobbled it up in one go.

"Easy, boy, you don't want to choke yourself."

"Morning," the jackdaw replied.

Alice put the gravy boat on the table and sat down.

"Cheers." She raised the port to her lips and took a sip. "This is the bottle you bought me," Alice told her. "It's a very nice one."

"Happy birthday for yesterday." Taylor took a sip of her own. She wasn't used to port, and it had a rather odd taste, but it was quite pleasant. "Here's to many more."

"Thank you, dear. Now tuck in."

The port had gone straight to Taylor's head. She needed to eat something, pretty quickly, to neutralise the alcohol. She ate some beef. "This is delicious."

"It's a rare treat for me to have you here. I don't often have guests. I say you have to make the most of the company you can get at my age."

"You're not that old." Taylor's head was starting to spin. She had almost finished the port.

"I'm old enough. Old enough to know what's important."

"And what's that?" Taylor was feeling quite drunk now. Her own voice sounded slurred.

"The status quo. Keeping things normal. That's what's important. As you get older and you start to count the days you have left and you do what you can to make sure you keep things the same."

"You're probably right." For some reason she'd started to giggle. "Sorry, this port has gone right to my head."

"It's all right, love. It does you good to let go once in a while."

Taylor could see two plates of food in front of her now. Her eyelids sagged.

"Aren't you hungry?" Alice asked her. "You've barely touched your food."

"I feel strange. Suddenly very tired."

Her legs were now starting to go numb. Alice stood up and stared at her. The expression on her face was quite disturbing. It was a mixture of sympathy and something darker which Taylor couldn't put her finger on. She had never seen Alice look like this before.

"You saw the ring, didn't you?"

"What?" It was hard even to say that. It was taking all her energy just to stay conscious.

"Stanley's ring. You saw it in the drawer, didn't you?"

"No. No, I didn't."

"Liar. I won't have liars in my house."

"I think I'd better be going. I don't feel well."

"You'll go when I say so," Alice said. "I can't have anything upsetting the status quo. It was all a bit of a blur at first but when Milly saw Stanley's wedding ring, it all started to come back. But then I knew a clever girl like you was always going to do a bit of poking around. Did you enjoy the port?"

Taylor stared at the empty glass. "What have you done?"

Alice took out a bunch of keys and put them on the table. Taylor recognised her spare set. "You have trouble sleeping, don't you?"

Through the fog in her head, Taylor realised she'd been right about the missing sleeping tablets. How many had gone missing? Eight? Ten?

"Why?"

Alice watched her. "I didn't mean to kill him, you know. They ran around like headless chickens but none of them had a clue. It was quite funny. I can't have you ruining everything for me now. You're a clever one, Harriet Taylor, you'd have figured it out sooner or later. You did it sooner, but that isn't going to be a problem now."

"What do you mean?"

"You won't feel a thing. You really ought to wean yourself off those pills, you know. They'll be the death of you."

"Alice." Taylor's mouth was now incredibly dry. She was starting to drift off and she knew there was no way she could stop herself. She tried to concentrate and stay awake but it was no use. She could only just make out someone coming into the kitchen.

"Alice," she heard Eddie Sedgewick say, "that's enough. This can't carry on. Let's have a cup of tea and a chat."

Taylor watched, like she was in a dream, as Alice stood up, picked up the carving knife and went towards her next-door neighbour. Taylor tried to get up but her legs refused to obey her. She saw Eddie's mouth open but the words that came out made no sense. She saw Eddie pick up a frying pan from the sink and then everything went black.

CHAPTER FIFTY-SIX

"Welcome back, sleepyhead," DI Jack Killian said.

Taylor opened her eyes and flinched. The bright light hurt her. She looked at Killian and frowned.

"Where am I?" she croaked.

"Truro. You're in hospital. You gave us quite a fright back there."

"What day is it?"

"Wednesday. You were out for almost twenty-four hours."

"Where's Alice?" Flashes of what had happened at the old beekeeper's house started to come back to her.

"She's down at the station."

"What happened?"

"We got a call from a man called Eddie Sedgwick. He kept babbling on about something terrible happening at Alice Green's house. We got there as soon as we could. Eddie had a nasty knife wound to his shoulder. Alice was lying on the kitchen floor and you were unconscious at the dining table."

"What about Alice? She killed those three people."

"I know. She made a full confession. She'll be charged with the murders of Stanley Green, Milly Lancaster and

Dennis Albarn, as well as the attempted murder of Eddie Sedgwick."

"Is Eddie all right?"

"He'll be fine. He's quite handy with a frying pan."

"So it was — oh, I can't work this out." Taylor sat up in the bed and her vision went black for a few seconds. "So it was Alice, after all?"

"She told us everything. She killed Stanley Green by accident. Hit him with a shovel in a fit of rage. She panicked and buried his body in her garden and then somehow his hand worked its way out of the ground. Milly Lancaster saw it and she had to be silenced."

"What about Dennis Albarn?"

"He met up with Stanley the day before he was killed so he could've talked. When word got out that it was Stanley in the fishing nets, Alice had to shut Albarn up for good. She kept going on about the status quo and how it had to be preserved. She's a few bob short of a pound note, if you ask me."

"I still don't understand. How did she do it? She had us all fooled."

"She had DCI James fooled. He's not going to like this. He's been parading around in public saying all sorts of things about the Trotterdown police department and now he's going to come across as an idiot. Flummoxed by an old beekeeper."

Taylor smiled. *That's one consolation*, she thought.

"We got it all out of her. After Milly saw the finger, Alice had to act quickly. She suggested they go for a sunset trip up to Merryhead. They'd done it a few times before, so Milly didn't think there was anything amiss. They went in Milly's car. Alice bashed her brains in with a rock, jammed the locks and pushed the car over the cliff with Milly in it."

"And then she walked home? It's five miles."

"She's in good shape. She hid the screwdriver she used to jam the locks in Peter Sugden's bin and said just enough to make us suspect Sugden. The body in the garden was bothering her so she chopped it in half with a shovel and chucked the two pieces over Merryhead. It should have all worked out just fine for her, except that the fisherman was lucky enough to drag up the body in his nets."

"Lucky? Not sure that poor man would call it that. And what about Albarn?" Taylor's head was spinning. She still couldn't believe what had happened.

"She phoned Dennis Albarn from a payphone in Trotterdown and suggested they meet at his house. She said there was something in Stanley Green's will for him. She had him hook, line and sinker. He opened the door and Alice whacked him with the shovel before he had a chance to react. She dragged him inside, opened up the gas and left him there. The lightning strike later on was a stroke of luck. Then she hid the shovel in Albarn's shed."

"I feel like I've been dreaming these past few weeks," Taylor said. "It doesn't seem real."

"The scary part is this. She doesn't think she's done anything wrong. Besides Milly Lancaster, which she puts down to necessity, she's shown no remorse about any of it."

"But she called the police herself for Milly! What was going on there?"

"She really seems to have managed to convince herself for a while that she hadn't killed her. I think it only came back to her later. Maybe something triggered it for her?"

"Perhaps that's why she had that weird obsession with the honey. Remember how she kept saying there was something wrong with the honey? The bees like the bushes where she'd buried Stanley. There couldn't have been anything really wrong with it — it's hardly as if his body was starting to decompose so soon — but perhaps it was her way of dealing with it. Or repressing it. I feel such a fool. And I had her in my house!"

"We were all fooled. Some of us more than others."

"What will happen to her?"

"She'll probably spend the rest of her life in jail." Killian sighed. "Or a psychiatric unit. She'll give the shrinks a field day."

"Can I see her?"

"I don't think that's a good idea. She's not the sweet old beekeeper we thought she was. You got quite close to her, didn't you?"

"What about Eddie Sedgwick? What was he doing in Alice's house yesterday?"

"Eddie's the only person who suspected something all along. He's not as doddery as he comes across. He said he'd been watching Alice for quite some time and realised that something strange was going on. He saw your car there and decided to go and check to see if everything was all right. You were lucky. He may have saved your life."

Taylor swung her legs out of bed and stood up.

"What are you doing?" Killian said. "They'll want to keep you in for observation and you need to rest."

"I've been resting in here for twenty-four hours," Taylor said. "There's a holiday I need to take."

THE END

Thank you for reading this book. If you enjoyed it please leave feedback on Amazon, and if there is anything we missed or you have a question about then please get in touch. The author and publishing team appreciate your feedback and time reading this book.

Our email is office@joffebooks.com

www.joffebooks.com

22749481R00143

Printed in Great Britain
by Amazon